*"And just how w...
this mythical hu...*

She slanted a look toward Shane. "Shall I advertise for one or should I just go straight to that online site and say something to the effect that I'd like one husband, please. No chores will be required, no expertise necessary. Must be able to stand and look manly when so-called 'wife' deals with fire-breathing former in-laws."

She knew she sounded hysterical but she couldn't stop– she was spiraling out of control.

"Sounds like a piece of cake to me. How about you? Sound like a piece of cake to you? Or do you know something I don't about locating a husband who'd be a willing stand-in?"

"Not sure I understand what you mean by a stand-in," Shane said, "but I'd be willing."

"Willing?" she echoed, confused. "Willing to what?"

"I'd be willing to marry you so you could retain custody of Ricky."

Five sets of eyes turned to stare at him at the same time.

Dear Reader,

Welcome back to Ladera by the Sea, a charming
120-year-old family-run bed-and-breakfast in San Diego
with a breathtaking view of the Pacific Ocean. You might
recall meeting the family—Richard Roman and his four
daughters, Alexandra, Christina, Stephanie and Andrea,
in the first book, *Innkeeper's Daughter*. That book saw
oldest daughter workaholic Alex come to grips with her
true feelings for Wyatt Taylor, someone she had grown
up knowing and verbally sparring with for years. You've
returned just in time for their wedding. But, before that
can take place, second daughter Cris, the Inn's resident
chef, has to learn how to finally move past the heartache
of losing her first husband and recognize the love that's
been in her own backyard all along. Thrown into this is
a pending custody battle with her well-to-do former in-
laws who are suing for sole custody of her five-year-old
son, Ricky. Curious? Good. Come, read and I promise
that all secrets will be revealed.

As always, I thank you for taking the time to read my
book and from the bottom of my heart, I wish you
someone to love who loves you back.

All the best,

Marie Ferrarella

www.marieferrarella.com

Marie Ferrarella

A Wedding for Christmas

MILLS & BOON

Published in Great Britain 2014
by Mills & Boon, an imprint of Harlequin (UK) Limited,
Eton House, 18-24 Paradise Road, Richmond, Surrey, TW9 1SR

© 2014 Marie Rydzynski-Ferrarella

ISBN: 978 0 263 24482 3

33-0214

Harlequin (UK) Limited's policy is to use papers that are natural, renewable and recyclable products and made from wood grown in sustainable forests. The logging and manufacturing processes conform to the legal environmental regulations of the country of origin.

Printed and bound in Spain
by Blackprint CPI, Barcelona

MARIE FERRARELLA

is a USA TODAY bestselling and RITA® Award-winning author, and has written more than 240 books, some under the name Marie Nicole. As of January 2013, she has been published for 30 years. She earned a master's degree in Shakespearean comedy and, perhaps as a result, her writing is distinguished by humor and natural dialogue. Her goal is to entertain and to make people laugh and feel good. Her romances are beloved by fans worldwide. Visit her website, www.marieferrarella.com.

To
Nancy Diamond
&
Wendy Brower
For telling me
About their grandmother's
Azalea plant

PROLOGUE

SOMETIMES THE PATH from the family-owned bed-and-breakfast to the small, private cemetery that overlooked the sea seemed longer to reach than it actually was.

Other times, like today, he wasn't even aware of how long it took to get there. One second, Richard Roman was deciding that he wanted to share a few moments with his wife and his best friend, the next he was already standing before their headstones, talking to the two people who had known him the best and, just possibly, the longest.

His Amy had been in this spot overlooking the sea a long while—sometimes it felt as if she had *always* been here, whereas Daniel had been here only a little while. Richard missed them both so very much.

But it helped to come here to talk to them both whenever he was troubled or happy.

Someday, he himself would be laid to

rest here, Richard thought. Buried next to his Amy.

But not for many years to come.

His girls needed him.

The four of them, ranging in age from twenty-one to twenty-eight were well along on their journey into womanhood, but they still needed him, needed his guidance.

"Looks like Alex won't be wearing your wedding dress after all, Amy, even though she had her heart set on it. She's too tall and just a touch too curvy to get into it. I know that Wyatt has no complaints in that department, but Alex really did think she'd be walking down the aisle in your dress. She was very disappointed."

He shook his head, recalling the stricken look on Alex's face when she told him about the dress. "I know you're thinking," he continued, addressing Amy and Dan as though they were standing right in front of him, "that alternations can be made since the wedding isn't until Christmas, but Alex feels that it's disrespectful to alter the dress you wore when you married me. At times it's hard to believe it's Alex talking, but she's got this whole sensitive side to her that she never let on about." He chuckled. "Who knew, right, Dan?"

And then he smiled. The afternoon sun played along the planes of his face. "I guess your boy does bring out the best in Alex. None of us saw that coming," he confessed, then rethought his words. "Well, except for you, of course, Dan," he admitted. "You knew all along they were right for each other, didn't you? Otherwise, you wouldn't have insisted that Wyatt finish that book about the inn you started working on just before you died. If it hadn't been for that deathbed promise you extracted from Wyatt, Alex wouldn't be on the hunt for a wedding dress and my third offspring wouldn't be running around like a chicken without her head because Alex put her in charge of planning the reception. Cris, naturally, will be doing the cooking. Or rather, have the meal all ready for the reception right after the ceremony. If I know her, she'll be up all night the night before, getting everything prepared and just so. She is a perfectionist, our Cris. She takes after her mom," he added. "It's really a shame that her husband died so young. Michael was a great guy.

"Speaking of which," Richard said, interrupting himself, "one of Cris's old acquaintances, Shane McCallister is doing some renovation work on the inn for me. I've seen the way he eyes Cris when he thinks no one is watching. That young man is really taken with her. Who knows? There might just be a second wedding soon. I certainly hope so. Cris deserves to be happy, like Alex."

A wistful smile played on Richard's lips, and tears glimmered in his eyes as he looked from one headstone to the other. "I wish you both could be present for Alex and Dan's wedding. Yes, I know, you'll be here in spirit and that's an enormous comfort to your girls, but sometimes—" Richard dropped his voice to a whisper "—it would be nice to actually see you, touch you...."

He sighed as he glanced toward the rear of the inn. "I guess I'd better be getting back. I'll keep you posted on the search for Alex's wedding dress and on how everyone else is doing. I miss you both more than words can ever say."

He turned and made his way back to the

inn. Unlike the journey to the cemetery, the journey back always felt infinity longer, because he made it knowing he was all alone.

CHAPTER ONE

SHE SAW HER through the window.

Curious, Christina Roman MacDonald made her way to the garden. Her older sister, Alexandra, was just standing there, staring off into the horizon from the looks of it.

For most of her twenty-eight years, Alex had been the very definition of a workaholic, a veritable tribute to perpetual motion. Seeing her so still wasn't normal.

But then, this wasn't exactly a period of business as usual for her sister. Not with the all-important step she would be taking in just six short weeks.

"Having second thoughts?" Cris asked, coming up behind Alex.

The gardener, Silvio Juarez, had just finished mowing the lawn and the air was heavy with the scent of freshly cut grass.

Caught off guard, Alex whirled to find her sister standing behind her. "About?"

"Running for prom queen of Munchkin High," Cris said impatiently. Most brides-to-be lived and breathed wedding details this close to the event. Alex, apparently, was different. "About getting married, of course."

Alex merely shook her head. "All my doubts had come before Wyatt's proposal and I've long since worked them out of my system." Clearly, she was looking forward to being his wife.

"No, no second thoughts," she replied with a small, peaceful smile.

"Regrets, then?" Cris guessed, watching the set of Alex's shoulders. The two girls were closer than most. She could draw clues from Alex's body language. "Prewedding jitters?"

"No," Alex answered and then pointed out, "and it's too soon for prewedding jitters."

Cris laughed shortly. "Tell that to Stevi," she said. Of their younger sisters, Stephanie, two years Cris's junior, was the temperamental artistic one. "By the time your wedding day arrives, she'll have gone through three meltdowns. I've never seen her quite like this. At the very least, you'd think she was the one getting married, not you."

Alex gave a half shrug. Stevi tended to get caught up in whatever she was doing. The moment she'd heard that Alex was marrying Wyatt, she'd volunteered to handle all the details. Alex had been glad to have one less situation to deal with.

"Maybe she thinks that if it's not perfect, I'll hold it against her," Alex speculated. "She should know better."

"She should," Cris agreed, coming to stand beside Alex in the garden, "but you know Stevi. She's a bit of a drama queen when her nerves get strung out. Maybe you shouldn't have put her in charge of your wedding."

"As if I'd had a choice," Alex said with a smile. Stevi had commandeered the position. "Too late now. Besides, she was following me around on her knees until I finally gave in." She eyed Cris. "What would you have done?"

That was an easy one, Cris decided with a grin. "Eloped."

It was Alex's turn to laugh. "Right. Sorry, I forgot who I was talking to. The daughter who eloped and almost broke her father's heart."

"Don't exaggerate," Cris chided. "Dad knew the reason." And so did Alex. She'd met her late husband's parents at Mike's funeral, and although polite, they were so formal Alex had told Cris she was completely uncomfortable in their presence, something that rarely happened to her. "We did it so Mike wouldn't have to invite his parents to the ceremony and be forced to put up with them trying to talk him out of making 'a foolish mistake he'd regret for the rest of his life,' as they said."

"They were—and are—snobs and I'll always hold it against them that we didn't get to see you as a blushing bride," Alex said, immediately defensive on her sister's behalf. "Speaking of which…"

"Yes?" *Here it is,* Cris thought, the reason Alex was standing pensively out here rather than working at the front desk.

"I'm as calm about the wedding as a human being can be," she told Cris. "I feel like I'm finally getting it right." She pointed to the azalea bush that someone had given their father at their mother's funeral.

A healthy plant, it seemed to bloom at odd times, generally when something momentous was occurring in their lives.

This time, though, Cris took the words to mean that Alex felt she had been a screwup until a couple of months ago, whereas nothing could have been further from the truth.

"Don't run yourself down," Cris insisted. "You've been Dad's right hand—sometimes his left one, as well—for years now, running the inn when he was sick, being here day in, day out, no matter what else was going on. It even took you longer to graduate from University of San Diego because you were here all the time, performing feats of magic—"

Alex waved off her sister's accolades. "Not quite. And I wasn't talking about my work anyway. I meant the direction of my life."

She glanced around the garden and it seemed to her that despite the fact they were in San Diego, it *was* November, yet the garden was in full bloom. The sight filled her with joy.

"I always figured that running the inn would be it for me. You know, like being here would be the sole purpose of my life.

Making sure things ran smoothly while I watched you and Stevi and Andy get married, have kids. Grow," she added wistfully.

"Grow what? Fat?" Cris asked with a laugh.

Alex shook her head. "No, just grow. As women, as people," she elaborated, then added for good measure, "become multi-dimensional."

This *definitely* did not sound like the Alex Cris had grown up with. She scrutinized her sister.

"Are you feeling all righ? You're getting me a little uneasy. You're beginning to sound like some college professor OD'ing on Adlerian self-actualization. Besides," she added with a touch of asperity, "I didn't exactly 'grow' as a wife."

"That's because you weren't allowed to be one for very long," Alex reminded her. Cris and Mike were barely married before he was shipped out to Iraq, where his young life was cut short by a roadside sniper. The letter from Cris telling him she was pregnant was found in his breast pocket. "Next time will be better."

"Not going to be a next time," Cris informed her with quiet conviction.

Alex's mouth curved in a smile. "I think Shane's got other ideas on that subject," she said. They'd hired the general contractor for the latest renovations to the 120-year-old inn. Aside from excellent references, Shane McCallister was also the older brother of one of Cris's high school girlfriends.

Alex's pending nuptials had her evaluating everything around her with fresh eyes, and the way Shane was looking at Cris spoke volumes.

"Now you're babbling," Cris said dismissively, then eyed Alex. "This is your clever way of deflecting questions, isn't it?" she said, shaking her head. "I'm not prying, Alex, I was just being concerned about you."

"I'm fine," Alex replied with finality, calling an end to what she deemed an unnecessary discussion.

"Then what are you doing out here, communing with the azalea bush in the middle of the morning?" Cris didn't add that the behavior just wasn't like Alex, but her tone implied it.

Impatience creased Alex's brow. "It's called taking a break, Cris."

That was fine, except for one thing. "You don't take breaks."

"I didn't *used to* take breaks," Alex corrected. "This is the new, improved me." Alex smiled. "'The times, they are a-changin',' little sister," she added glibly. And then she glanced at her watch. Alex-in-Charge was back. "Shouldn't you be in the kitchen, working on lunch, using whatever time you have left before your three-foot assistant gets sprung from kindergarten? According to my calculations, Stevi should be picking Ricky up soon and bringing him home. Don't forget, Wyatt's back in L.A. for a week, so he's not here to play with your energized offspring and be his sidekick."

Cris knew she could count on her father to spend a little one-on-one time with his only grandchild. That was the good part about living at the inn with the rest of her family. Someone was always around to help out with Ricky when she was busy cooking.

"I did forget," Cris confessed. "But have you worked out the logistics yet?"

"What logistics?"

"Where you and Wyatt will live after the ceremony?"

"Here," Alex said with finality. "Where else would we live?"

Granted Wyatt had grown up spending summers at the inn with his father, but a lot of men would have wanted to begin their marriage in a place of their own. "Well, Wyatt does have that house in Brentwood."

To Cris, Alex had always had an answer for everything. Now was no different. "Where he'll stay when he can't avoid being in L.A. Otherwise, we've got dibs on the new section being added to the inn. Whenever your guy gets around to finishing it, that is."

"He's not my guy," Cris protested, even as a bit of color climbed her cheeks, highlighting her embarrassment. "You hired him."

"You knew him," Alex countered.

"That has nothing to do with anything," Cris declared. At the time, they'd needed a general contractor and giving her old friend's brother a job seemed the right thing to do. Her father and Alex made those kinds of decisions, so her input wouldn't have carried much weight, Cris told herself.

But Alex had a different take on the situation. "Your knowing Shane helped seal the deal," she told Cris.

Cris couldn't help wondering if there was a reason Alex was laying this at her doorstep. If so, her sister was overlooking one obvious fact.

"Ha. He could have been Santa Claus, and if you hadn't liked his references and his plans for the extension, you wouldn't have hired him and you know it."

"Let's just say you have a point. Meanwhile, break—not that it actually turned out to be that—is over, and I've got to be getting back to the front desk. I left Dorothy in charge and you know how much she dislikes being in a position of authority."

Cris smiled sympathetically. She herself didn't exactly care for manning the front desk, although she was getting better at it.

As for Dorothy, she was one of her father's lost souls, people who occasionally turned up at the inn. Their father would extend a helping hand until that person could stand on his or her own two feet.

Dorothy, her life in shambles, had come to them years back. She'd booked a room for one night so that she'd spend her last night on earth in a place with clean sheets and the smell of the sea through the opened window. Sensing her hopelessness and desperation, Richard Roman had stayed up all night with her, talking about everything and anything. When dawn finally arrived, the world somehow didn't seem quite so bleak for the woman.

Because she confessed that she couldn't pay for the room and she wouldn't take charity, Richard gave her a job. That allowed Dorothy to keep her dignity. The job turned into a vocation and she worked her way up. She became head housekeeper—and was fiercely devoted and loyal to Richard and his four daughters.

As they walked into the front room, Dorothy immediately released a sigh of relief. She moved away from the desk as if the floor had suddenly caught on fire and she was barefoot.

"You act as though you didn't expect me to come back," Alex remarked, amused.

Now that Alex had returned, Dorothy could be a little magnanimous. "Of course

I did. It's just that those were the longest twenty minutes I've ever spent."

"Don't understand how," Alex commented, "seeing as I was only gone for fifteen. And I would have been back sooner, but Cris just kept talking and talking." She slanted a sideways glance at her sister, then added with a completely straight face, "Didn't seem right, cutting her off and walking away just like that."

"No, of course not," Dorothy agreed solemnly. "I wouldn't have expected you to."

"She's pulling your leg, Dorothy," Cris said. There was never any winning with Alex. "You are impossible. I should start composing my letter of condolence to Wyatt now. Better yet, I should tell him to run for the hills while he still can."

"Don't you dare," Stevi warned, entering with Cris's five-year-old son in tow. "You do anything to mess up this wedding I've been working so hard on and I swear, it'll be the last thing you ever do." Stevi's eyes narrowed as her threat became more menacing. "Alex and Wyatt are getting married Christmas Day if I have to hog-tie both of them and pull them up to the altar in a horse-drawn cart."

"Nothing weird about that statement." Alex laughed, shaking her head. "Maybe I *should* elope."

"You do and I'll hunt you both down and make you pay dearly for my pain and suffering," Stevi warned.

Threatening vibes were all but wafting from Stevi's five-six form. "You do realize," Alex said, "that you're just organizing a small wedding reception and not staging the second invasion of Normandy or a military coup in a third-world country, right?"

"What I *realize*," Stevi responded, "is that you have no concept of what's involved in carrying off a successful reception."

Alex extended a sympathetic smile and an offer she knew would be refused. "If it's too much for you, Stevi, I'll gladly relieve you of the responsibility."

Stevi's blue eyes widened with complete surprise. "You wouldn't dare," she breathed.

Alex chuckled as she shook her head. "I can't decide if you just uttered a frantic plea or tossed out a challenge without remembering to throw down the symbolic glove."

Stevi blew out a breath, doing her best to rein herself in. "Okay, maybe I am being a little intense," she allowed.

Alex's eyes met Stevi's, pinning her where she stood. "Maybe?"

Stevi relented. "Okay, I *am* being a little intense—"

"Only in the sense that World War II was a 'little' conflict. Stevi, I love you, but get a grip. This is just supposed to be a small gathering."

"There's nothing small about three hundred people in my book."

"What three hundred people?" Alex inquired incredulously. Her list had under a hundred people on it. *Well* under a hundred. "Are you throwing the doors open to the general population?"

"No," Stevi insisted. "I'm just counting Wyatt's list."

"Wyatt's got over two hundred people coming?" she asked.

"That's how many names are on his final list." Stevi nodded. "Wyatt pared it down from five hundred," she added. "He didn't want you to be overwhelmed."

"Too late," Alex retorted.

"How could you and Wyatt not have discussed the invite list?" Cris asked her in disbelief.

"Well, I…just assumed he was…leaving this to me…" Alex trailed off. "His work has kept him away from the inn a lot. Say, Stevi, when did he have time to—"

"Now, Miss Alex," Dorothy interrupted loyally. "You only get married for the first time once."

"Wyatt knows I don't want the wedding to get out of hand or come off like a three-ring circus. It's supposed to be more or less an intimate gathering. Why is he inviting the immediate world? I want to see the list, Stevi."

"I don't have it with me," her sister protested. "I went to pick up Ricky, remember?"

"I can wait," Alex said matter-of-factly, indicating that she expected her to retrieve the list—now.

Stevi lifted her chin. "You don't believe me? Or is it Wyatt you're asking me to check up on?"

"Yes" was Alex's answer. "Now go get the list."

CHAPTER TWO

"MAMA."

Cris looked down at her son. Throughout the discussion about the guest list, Ricky had been trying to get her attention by pulling on the apron that had become practically a part of every outfit she put on.

As resident chef, she spent most of her time preparing her kitchen, preparing her menu or preparing the meals themselves for the ever-changing array of guests, who came as much for the meals as they did for the inn's charm, service and beautiful view.

Impatience vibrated in her five-year-old's plaintive cry.

"What is it, little man?" Cris asked, placing her hands on his slight shoulders.

"I want to show you something," Ricky told her with enthusiasm on the brink of exploding.

Though he was clearly bursting to share

whatever it was, Cris knew that her son liked being coaxed. So she played along and asked, "What is it, Ricky?"

"I drewed you a picture," he said proudly as he began digging into his bright blue-and-white backpack with its cheerful cartoon character logo—a gift from Dorothy on his first day of school.

"Drew," Cris automatically corrected. "You *drew* a picture."

Ricky spared her a glance as if he didn't see what the problem was. "That's what I said," he insisted. "I drewed you a picture. Teacher told us to make one of our family."

Cris opened her mouth to try to make the five-year-old understand the difference between the word he used and the word he was *supposed* to use, but decided to temporarily suspend the grammar lesson when she saw the picture he'd "drewed."

At times, she still couldn't help marveling that she was his mother. She certainly felt less than qualified for the position. Her own image of a mother—based on what she remembered of *her* mother—was that of unshakable wisdom mixed with love and understanding. While she had more than endless amounts of love to shower on the boy and she thought of herself as an understanding person, she felt sorely lacking in the unshakable wisdom department.

Every day seemed a challenge and there were days when she felt she'd made wrong choices. Very simply, there were more than a few days when she felt she didn't know what she was doing.

Though there was nothing she wanted more than to be Ricky's mother, she couldn't shake the feeling that every step she took in this unfamiliar land called motherhood was like walking in a field riddled with pools of quicksand. Any second now, she expected to take the wrong step and be sucked under.

There were other times, though, when gazing down into the happy little face that seemed the perfect combination of Mike's features and her own, that she felt she had to be doing *something* right because just look at how Ricky was turning out. He was wonderfully well adjusted.

Of course, Cris was the first one to point out that she wasn't doing it alone. She had a fabulous support system that consisted of her father and her sisters, even Wyatt and his late father, Dan, whom they had all referred to as "Uncle Dan" even though he really wasn't related to them. They all doted on Ricky, filling his world with love and watching over him to make sure that no harm ever came to him.

Every night, without fail, Cris thanked God for her family and for bringing Ricky into her life. Without the boy, she didn't know how she would have survived the sudden, heart-destroying loss of her husband.

"Hey, you didn't tell me you had a picture," Stevi cried, pretending her feelings were hurt as she walked into the kitchen.

Of the four sisters, only Stevi had artistic abilities—not to mention occasionally the artistic temperament that went with them. She was creating recognizable drawings by the time she was four and was still inclined to find an artistic outlet for her talent rather than joining Alex and Cris in making Ladera-by-the-Sea her life's work.

"That's 'cause I wanted to show Mama first," Ricky informed his aunt with all the confidence of a child who believed himself to be the well deserving center of his family's universe. To everyone's credit—

including his own—he was neither spoiled nor truly self-centered. Kindness came naturally to him, tempering most things that he said. "But it's okay for you to look now, 'cause I showed it to her."

He unfolded the drawing and held it up for his mother to see. Stevi and Alex shifted over toward Cris to view it, as well.

"Do you like it?" Ricky asked, his blue eyes eager and shining as he looked at his mother. "It's us," he added, just in case she'd missed what he said about it being a drawing of his family.

How silly, Cris chided herself, to get choked up over a crayon drawing, even a good crayon drawing, depicting a little boy holding what she could only assume was his mother's hand. The two figures were surrounded by three female figures and a tall, thin man, who, because Ricky had used a gray crayon for the hair, had to be his grandfather. This was their family, Cris thought, the way her son saw all of them.

Close.

Hovering over this gathering was what appeared to be a large, unusual-looking bird.

Cris glanced at her son. Approval and maternal pride shone in her eyes.

"It's beautiful, honey."

Ricky nodded, as if he had expected that response. Proudly, he acted like a tour guide for the drawing. "That's you, Mama, and me. You're holding my hand—"

"I can see that," Cris said, relieved that she had correctly assumed as much and sounded believable when she commented on it.

"—'cause I'm letting you," Ricky added by way of a narrative. "But I am a big boy."

Cris knew that was her son's way of making sure she understood he considered himself independent. "Yes, you are," she agreed.

"And that's Aunt Alex, and Aunt Stevi and Aunt Andy," he continued, pointing his finger at each figure. All three had blond hair, just as he and his mother did, but he had dressed them in different colors and had managed to capture the height difference. "And that's Grandpa," he explained, jabbing a small finger at the other male on the page. "And that's Daddy," Ricky concluded, pointing to the winged creation just above his self-portrait.

"You drew your daddy as a bird?" Alex

asked, trying to follow her nephew's reasoning.

"Not a *bird*," Ricky said indignantly. "He's an angel."

"Of course he is. Can't you see that?" Stevi deliberately took her nephew's side, pretending that Alex had to be blind not to see the figure for who it was.

Cris laughed as she bent over to hug her son, delighted that he thought his father was watching over him, the way she'd explained when Ricky had asked her to tell him about his father.

"Yes, he is, Ricky. Don't mind your aunt Alex, she's not good at seeing what's right in front of her unless someone points it out."

Alex knew Cris was referring to the antagonistic relationship Alex and Wyatt had had on the surface for years before Alex had realized how deep the feelings ran. Because Ricky was present, she decided not to comment on Cris's barely veiled allusion.

"You gonna put that on the 'frigerator?" Ricky asked, eagerly shifting from foot to foot as he watched his mother's face.

"Yes, I am." She held out the drawing, taking note of its size. It was bigger than most of the drawings he brought home. "But you realize that means I have to take down another one of your drawings," she reminded Ricky. "We've only go so much room on the refrigerator—even if it is industrial-sized," she added, winking at him affectionately.

The boy nodded solemnly. "I know, Mama. I'm not a dummy-head."

"Ah, a new term from the playground I see," Cris noted with a good-natured sigh. He seemed to have a new addition to his vocabulary at least once a week. Usually not of the best variety. "No, sweetheart, you're not a 'dummy-head' and I hope you don't call anyone else that," she added, eyeing the boy.

Silky straight blond hair swung as Ricky shook his head in firm denial. "No, 'cause you said not to call people names even if they call me those names. Right?" he asked.

"Right. Because that makes you the bigger man," Cris concluded firmly.

An unexpected little frown formed on Ricky's forehead as he said, "Teacher says I'm not a man."

Alex ruffled her nephew's hair and laughed affectionately. "Your teacher doesn't know you the way we do," she assured the boy. "You're more of a man than some guys three times your age."

From the look on Ricky's face, her nephew clearly saw no reason to contest that. He beamed at her as though she had just lifted a bad spell he'd been forced to endure for the sake of peace and quiet.

"You hungry, big guy?" Cris asked.

"Uh-huh," he answered, once again bobbing his head.

"Okay, let's see what we can find for you to eat," Cris suggested.

As she slipped her arm around his shoulders, ready to usher him to the inn's kitchen, Shane McCallister emerged from the section of the inn temporarily curtained off with sheets of plastic. They hung from the ceiling and went all the way to the floor to keep dust spreading to the rest of the inn at a minimum.

Behind the plastic sheets, the latest addition, as well as renovations to a previously constructed section, was taking place. Dust from his recent foray into carpentry had turned sections of Shane's dark blond hair to a shade of off-white.

Ricky had taken to Shane astoundingly

fast. Excited to see him now, the boy broke away from his mother and ran over to the contractor.

"Look at what I drewed, Shane!" he declared proudly, holding up the drawing.

Shane got down on one knee, the hammer that was hanging from his tool belt hitting the tiled floor with a thud. He gave the boy his complete attention.

One arm around the boy's waist, Shane pulled Ricky to him as he held one edge of the drawing with the other. "You drew this?" he asked with the appropriate amount of wonder in his voice.

Pleased at the reaction he was receiving, Ricky grinned. "Yes, I did."

"Cool. That's a really fine family portrait," Shane said. Releasing Ricky but still holding the drawing with one hand, he pointed with the other hand to what had previously been identified as a bird. "That angel your dad?"

Cris exchanged looks with Stevi, who watched from a distance. The latter shrugged in confusion, as clueless as Cris about how Shane could identify what still appeared to be an oversize bird. Cris couldn't help wondering if perhaps Shane had somehow overheard the end of the conversation about the drawing. Shane's startling interpretative ability seemed too much of a coincidence otherwise.

"Yes!" Ricky cried out, glancing over his shoulder at his mother. The glance all but shouted, *See?*

"You can tell it's an angel?" Cris asked, gazing at the general contractor pointedly to see if he was pulling her leg.

"Sure," Shane replied, the complete picture of innocence.

"Why didn't you think it was a bird?" she asked suspiciously.

He regarded her as if the answer was obvious. "Because it's a family portrait and Ricky doesn't have a pet bird."

Cris laughed as she shook her head. "You're good," she told him, impressed. "You make it sound so simple."

The smile on his handsome, tanned face was utterly and frustratingly enigmatic. "Some things just are. Right, Rick?"

In response to hearing the adult version of his name, Ricky puffed up his small chest and beamed at this newest man in his life.

"Right," he echoed with confidence. "Mama's gonna make me lunch. You wanna have some, too?" Ricky asked, slipping his hand into Shane's as if the man's affirmative answer was already a foregone conclusion.

"Okay," Shane readily agreed. He jerked a thumb toward where he'd parked his vehicle. "I was just going to take break and get my lunch out of the truck. Give me a few minutes and I'll join you, Rick," he said, pulling his hand out of the boy's grip.

Cris stared at him. "You're brown-bagging it?" she asked, incredulously.

Granted the addition and the renovations had been going on for more than a week now, but to be honest, she hadn't been all that aware where Shane and the men he sometimes had working for him took their meals. She'd assumed he was out in the dining area.

"Yeah," he answered. "It saves time if I don't have to drive over to one of those fast-food places. This way, I get done faster and I can spend the rest of the time working on the addition."

A lot had been going on at the inn of late, what with Alex and Wyatt's wedding swiftly approaching and Ricky beginning kindergarten, not to mention a mini-convention of historical writers coming to the inn to hold this year's annual meeting. Consequently, Cris had been exceedingly busy, aware only that Shane had been in and out of the inn several times to take measurements and render estimates after being apprised of what their father and Alex wanted done.

She realized now that he'd only really been on the job a few days.

She had to focus, Cris upbraided herself. Otherwise, she wouldn't be able to get done all the things done she needed to.

No time like the present, she decided.

"Saves more time if you just tell me what you'd like to eat and I make it for you," she said with an easy smile.

A smile he found more than captivating.

He always had.

Even so, or perhaps because it was so, he shook his head, brushing off her generous suggestion. "No, that's okay. You're busy."

She raised a perfectly arched eyebrow. "And you're not?"

He wasn't clear on what one thing had to do with the other. After all, this wasn't a competition where the loser would wait on the winner. "Well, yeah, I am, but—"

"No buts," she informed him. "You're coming with us to the kitchen."

"Yeah!" Ricky added his minuscule weight to the argument.

Then, to ensure that Shane would indeed comply with his and his mother's wishes, Ricky once again slipped his small hand into the contractor's callused one. Holding on with all his might, Ricky gave Shane's hand as hard a tug as he could manage.

"Wow." Shane lunged just enough to make it seem he'd been thrown off balance by the boy. "You sure are strong." He pretended to eye the boy suspiciously. "You work out?"

Ricky giggled and shook his head, obviously pleased with the evaluation. "No. I'm strong 'cause Mama feeds me good."

"I bet she does," Shane agreed, glancing in Cris's direction, a trace of his admiration showing through. "But just so you get it right the next time, what you should say is Mama feeds me well," Shane explained, gently correcting the little boy's grammar.

Her momentary connection with Shane's intense dark blue eyes instantly quickened Cris's pulse at the same time that his thoughtful method of correcting her son's grammar gladdened her heart. She was always partial to people who were nice to Ricky.

"She feeds you good, too?" Ricky asked, surprised.

Cris did her best to stifle the laugh that rose to her lips, but Shane, she noticed, didn't attempt to hide his reaction.

Instead, he laughed. "You're going to be a challenge, I can see. Tell you what, maybe after I knock off for the day, you and I can find some time for a little grammar lesson."

Excitement all but radiating from him, Ricky asked as he continued to tug the man to the kitchen, "Who are you gonna knock off?"

"No, not who," Shane corrected. "What."

That threw Ricky back into confusion. "You're gonna knock off a what?" he asked, his thin, wheat-colored eyebrows knotting; he was clearly perplexed.

Shane laughed, charmed and delighted. "You are definitely going to be a challenge," he told the boy as they crossed the kitchen threshold. "But it'll give me a chance to practice my skills."

"Practice what skills?" Cris inquired as she crossed to the refrigerator with the picture Ricky had drawn.

"Teaching skills," Shane replied. When she looked at him quizzically, he explained, "I've got a teaching degree, and I majored in English."

"I didn't know that." Something didn't make sense. "So why aren't you teaching?"

That was easy enough to explain. "Jobs aren't exactly plentiful these days, even for teachers. And there's no reason for you to know that I got a degree in teaching. You and I kind of lost touch after high school," he reminded her.

They had at that. By then, she'd been going with Mike, and Shane had just been the older brother of one of her girlfriends, a guy she'd dated a couple of times before Mike had come into her life and swept her off her feet.

Seeing Shane again after all this time, she fleetingly wondered how things would have turned out if he had swept her off her feet instead. Burying the question that could never really be answered, Cris forced a smile to her lips as she opened the refrigerator and cheerfully asked, "Okay, men, what'll it be?"

CHAPTER THREE

RICKY SCRAMBLED UP onto one of the stools that stood against the long stainless-steel service table where Cris did most of her food preparations. Rather than sit, he knelt on the stool so that he appeared bigger to his new friend, who took the stool next to his.

"You know what I like, Mama," Ricky piped up in response to her question.

Like everyone else in the family, she indulged her son, but not when it came to his nutrition. "Yes, I do, and you know what I say to that."

"What?" Shane asked, the exchange arousing his curiosity. He glanced from Cris to her son. "What is it you like, Rick?"

"Hot dogs!" the boy declared, his high-pitched voice all but vibrating with enthusiasm. Cris had a strong feeling that if she allowed it, the boy would eat hot dogs for breakfast, lunch and dinner. "I love 'em best of all!"

"I like them myself," Shane told Ricky, getting a big grin from the boy and a reproving glare from his somewhat frustrated mother. "But you know," he continued without missing a beat, taking his cue from the expression on Cris's face, "they're really not very good for your insides. That's why they should only be eaten on very, very special occasions. Right, Rick?"

The boy appeared torn between siding with his newfound friend, whom he wanted to impress, and campaigning for his beloved meal of choice. When Shane continued eyeing him as if waiting for backup from an equal, Ricky finally capitulated, shrugging his small, thin shoulders as he did so.

"Yeah, I guess so."

"You know what else I like, Ricky?" Shane asked the boy.

There was a wary look in the child's eyes as he inquired, "What?"

Shane leaned in closer and ruffled the boy's hair affectionately. "Vegetables."

Ricky appeared horrified at the mere

thought. "Oh, yuck." The response rose to his lips automatically.

Shane pretended to consider what he'd said. "Well, maybe they don't taste quite as good as hot dogs," he allowed, "but they do taste pretty good. I like them mashed in with potatoes, or fried with a little oil and bread crumbs. And not only do they taste good," he continued, focusing exclusively on Ricky rather than on his mother, "but they help make your insides healthy and they make you strong. Pretty cool, huh?"

Ricky regarded him with eyes beyond huge. "They really make you strong?"

"They really make you strong," Shane echoed. He gazed at Ricky solemnly and drew his thumb across his chest in the form of an X. "Cross my heart," he told the boy.

Ricky shifted on the stool, planting his seat on the plastic cushion, and looked up at his mother. "Can we have that, Mama? Can we have vegeta-bib-bles with mashed potatoes and bread crumbs?"

"No," Shane said, laughing and jumping in to correct him, "it's either with mashed potatoes *or* fried with bread crumbs." It occurred to him that maybe he had overstepped his boundaries. Turning to Cris, Shane tendered a veiled apology. "I didn't mean to put you out."

"You didn't," she assured him quickly. "Trust me, any suggestion that'll get this one—" she nodded at Ricky "—to eat his vegetables is greatly appreciated. Any particular vegetable I should be using?"

Shane thought only a moment, remembering the combination his mother used to make to get his elder brother and him to eat their vegetables. "Well, how about spinach? That goes pretty well with mashed potatoes."

"Spinach?" Ricky cried, clutching his throat and pretending to fall over, poisoned, while emitting a rasping noise that, Shane assumed, was supposed to be a death rattle.

Shane laughed at the impromptu performance. "Oh, most definitely spinach," he told Ricky with certainty. "That makes you *really* strong. You ever hear of Popeye the Sailor?"

"Uh-uh," Ricky said, shaking his head so hard that if he'd been a cartoon character, his head would have gone spinning off.

The boy's answer didn't surprise Shane.

He was convinced that kids today were missing out on a very special collection of imaginative cartoons from a classic era.

"No?" he said, pretending to question. "Well, have I got a treat for you. Why don't I tell you all about him while your mom makes us lunch?"

She had to hand it to Shane. He was handling her son like a pro. She caught herself wondering if Shane had gotten married. He wasn't wearing a wedding ring, but then a lot of men didn't. And he seemed like such a natural with kids it was difficult for her to imagine that he'd gotten that way without having one of his own to practice on.

The thought of Shane having a family made her happy for him, but at the same time, it came with an accompanying sense of…well, sadness, for lack of a better word.

"Anything else you two men would like to go with those vegetables?" Cris asked, doing her very best not to laugh.

Shane shrugged casually. "Anything you've got will be fine."

"Yeah, fine, Mama," Ricky said, emulating Shane.

"How about fried chicken?" she suggested.

Rather than agree, Shane first looked at the boy to have him weigh in. "What do you say—you up for that, Rick?"

This time, Ricky bobbed his head with the same enthusiasm he'd displayed when asking for hot dogs.

"Fried chicken it is," Shane told Cris, placing their "order."

"One last question," Cris promised. "Light meat or dark?" The question was for Shane, since she already knew which her son preferred.

"I'm a leg man myself," Shane said with a hint of a smile that made Cris think perhaps the information applied to more than chickens.

"Me, too, Mama," Ricky piped up right after Shane. "I'm a leg man, too."

Cris banked the urge to hug Ricky to her and laugh. She knew that would only embarrass him before his new hero. But resisting the desire wasn't easy.

"Two orders of fried chicken drumsticks coming up," Cris told Shane and her son.

Ricky turned his attention back to Shane.

"Who's this sailor guy you said eats spinach?" he prodded. His expression clearly indicated he thought that *anyone* willing to eat the weed was less than a hero type, as well as somewhat weird.

With a smile, Shane proceeded to tell the little boy a story the way he recalled it from watching Saturday-television when he was about Ricky's age.

As she listened to Shane, Cris concluded that the man was as wrapped up in the story as the boy was.

HE HAD A gift, Cris thought.

She'd gone to work the moment Shane had pulled his stool closer to Ricky's and started telling the boy an elaborate story complete with a villain, a fair damsel in distress and the green seaweedlike vegetable that turned a somewhat aging sailor into almost a superhero with inflated forearms. Spinach gave the sailor, Popeye, the ability to pummel his enemy into the ground while rescuing a damsel only the one-eyed hero could love.

Cris caught herself listening to the details on more than one occasion as she prepared their lunches. It got to the point that she had to order herself to concentrate so as to block out Shane's storytelling.

She noticed that Shane timed his story to finish almost at the exact same moment that she announced, "Lunch is ready."

She placed both plates on the shiny stainless-steel counter, then slid one in front of Shane and the other in front of her son.

Ricky gazed at the vegetable combination a little uneasily, then raised his eyes to see what his newly discovered idol would do.

When Shane dug in, Ricky obviously felt compelled to follow suit, which he did, albeit reluctantly and in what seemed like slow motion. The first bite he took of the mashed potatoes and spinach combination produced a surprised expression on his small, angular face. His eyes looked ready to pop out. "Hey, this is good," he told Shane.

Which was exactly the way Shane had reacted the first time *he'd* taken a bite. Ricky, Shane decided, reminded him somewhat of himself.

"Told you," Shane said to the boy with a wide, satisfied smile.

Through hooded eyes, Cris watched in amazement as her son ate the spinach and potatoes she'd made for him. She expected him to leave at least half on his plate, but he ate until it was all gone. Not a moment's hesitation, not a myriad of sour faces above his plate and certainly no begging or bargaining the way there usually was when Ricky faced something he would as soon walk away from than eat.

Ricky cleared his plate just as his hero did, then, still emulating Shane, pushed the plate back and patted his stomach.

"That was very good," Shane told Cris.

"Yeah, very good," Ricky echoed gleefully, emitting a huge, satisfied sigh the way Shane had half a minute ago.

"Well, I've got to be getting back to the job before your sister starts thinking she's hired a freeloader."

"What's a freeloader?" Ricky wanted to know, looking from Shane to his mother for an answer.

"Something Mr. McCallister is definitely not," Cris assured her son with certainty. The man more than earned his pay—in all departments. Her eyes met Shane's and she murmured, "Thank you."

The corners of his mouth curved ever so

slightly as Shane said, "There's no need to thank me."

And with that, he left the kitchen.

Two sets of eyes watched him until he'd completely disappeared from view.

"THAT WAS NOTHING short of a miracle. I just wanted you to know that," Cris said later on that day. Taking a break from her kitchen duties, she'd sought Shane out and found him exactly where he was supposed to be— hip deep in renovations. He was standing with his back toward her, intent on what he was doing on the workbench.

Coming up behind Shane, she was careful not to startle him. She didn't want to be responsible for him making any unintentional cuts in either his project *or* himself.

Shane was running a power sander over the plank he intended to use for a new floorboard to match the ones throughout the inn, and he had on a mask to cut down on inhaling the dust.

Cris patiently waited until he'd stopped running the sander before she spoke again, knowing she'd either have to shout to be heard or get in his way so he could see her. Just waiting him out was simpler.

Turning the moment he heard her voice, Shane put the sander back down on the workbench he'd set up and lowered the mask from his nose and mouth.

He looked a little like a surgeon operating in the middle of a sandstorm, Cris thought with an unbidden wave of something that felt very close to affection.

"Excuse me?" he said, fairly certain he'd heard her wrong.

"A miracle," she reiterated. "You performed a miracle," she added in a clear, unshakable voice. "We could call it the miracle of the spinach and mashed potatoes, or just call it Shane's Miracle for short," she said, really grinning at him this time.

For a second, Shane watched in pure fascination as Cris's smile coaxed the dimples in her cheeks to emerge, making her look even more appealing—something he hadn't thought possible until he witnessed it himself.

He cocked his head a bit uncertainly. "Are you talking about lunch?"

"I'm talking about my son, the vegetable hater, eagerly eating spinach. To get him to eat *any* kind of a vegetable, I've tried to bribe him, coax him, do everything short of threatening to leave him wandering in Sea-World on his own for a week, and you get him to do it in under ten minutes.

Cris shook her head in admiration. "You really must have been *some* teacher," she told him with genuine awe.

His answering smile carried a bit of irony. "Never really had the chance to flex my muscles, so to speak," he said. "I got my degree and suddenly found that I could only get substitute teaching jobs where all they wanted was for me to be a glorified babysitter." The trace of bitterness she also heard in his voice surprised her. Shane seemed like such a laid-back character, someone who let stress roll off him. "When I started teaching the kids, I wound up ruffling a few feathers, and the jobs, never really plentiful to begin with, started not coming at all," he finished with an air of disbelief even now.

"Well, the world lost a fantastic teacher the day you were forced to walk away," she assured him. "If I was in charge of a school, I'd want all my teachers to be like you. You really connected with Ricky, right from the start," she marveled. "I mean, he's a friendly little guy, but it does take a bit for him to warm up to a person. With you he showed all the signs of love at first sight."

Shane self-consciously shrugged off the compliment, not willing to accept what he felt wasn't rightfully his. "Maybe he just wants a male to connect with and I happened to be handy."

"You might have been handy, but Ricky's already 'connected' to my dad and he gets along well with Wyatt, Alex's fiancé. He really wasn't looking for a male role model or someone to act as a father figure. Nope, Ricky just took to you exceptionally quickly," Cris told him.

Again he shrugged. He didn't care to have a spotlight shone on him no matter what his accomplishment.

"Must be my winning personality," he quipped.

She laughed, not because his personality *wasn't* engaging, but because his humor was so droll.

"Must be," she agreed. "Anyway, I just wanted to thank you. You've officially cracked the impenetrable vegetable ceiling," she told him, amusement curving her mouth. "I was expecting him to turn green or look around for somewhere to 'deposit' his mouthful of spinach. Instead, he not only swallowed what was in his mouth, but polished off what was on his plate."

"I know, I was there," Shane said with a wink.

Not for the first time, Cris felt something quicken inside her in response and silently argued it was because she'd forgotten to eat again, the way she did all too often when she got involved with what she was doing.

She began to back away. "Well, thank you for being there."

"Hey, anytime. Let me know if you have more trouble getting Ricky to eat his vegetables. Or doing his homework, for that matter," Shane added, warming up to the subject. "I'm still awed that kids in kindergarten actually *get* homework. If he has any trouble at all—not that I think he will," Shane quickly interjected in case Cris thought he was impugning Ricky's mental capabilities. "But if he hits a snag while I'm here, let me know. As much as I enjoy working with my hands, I miss the challenge of finding new ways to get kids interested in what I have to teach."

"Ah, a builder and a scholar," she said. "I guess that qualifies you as a Renaissance man."

"Either that or just a guy eager to earn a living and stay ahead of the bill collectors," he joked.

Still grateful beyond words for the breakthrough, Cris wanted to show him how thankful she was.

The only thing she had to give was food—so she did.

"Listen, when you're ready to turn in your tool belt and call it a day," she said, waving at the work he was doing, "instead of just leaving, why don't you come by the dining area for dinner. On the house," she added. "The very least I can do is keep you fed."

There was no need for that, he thought. He didn't want her feeling she owed him, especially for doing something he enjoyed: telling stories and getting kids to come around. Ricky seemed like an exceptionally intelligent boy and was incredibly easy to talk to.

Getting through to him hadn't been a real challenge, just a pleasant diversion.

"I like paying my own way," he told her.

Cris looked at him pointedly. "I guess we're alike, because so do I."

CHAPTER FOUR

ORDINARILY, CRIS WOULD have retreated at this point. She had never been known as the pushy sister—that title belonged to Alex. But for some reason, she caught herself digging in.

If asked, she wouldn't have been able to explain why—she just knew she should.

So she did.

"Correct me if I'm wrong here," she told Shane, "but you do have to eat at some point later on today, right?" Her eyes challenged his as she waited for him to reply.

A half smile curved his mouth because she'd managed to amuse him. "Right."

As she recalled, he had been very logical as a teen, so she was approaching this evening meal issue as logically as she could. "Do you cook?"

Shane laughed outright before answering. "If I have to."

"So your dinner is often what—takeout?" she asked.

But the moment the words were out of her mouth, she suddenly realized she was assuming things again, assuming he was single.

What if he wasn't?

"I'm sorry," she murmured, her voice hardly above a whisper. Distressed, she wished that she'd thought before speaking or, better yet, that the ground would just open up and swallow her whole.

"For?" he prompted, not following her.

"I just assumed you weren't married and… Never mind," she concluded uneasily, feeling that anything she said from there on in would just worsen the situation. She felt she finally understood the meaning of the phrase "sticking your foot in your mouth." "Ever since I lost Mike, I just see everyone else in the same situation," she apologized. "Without a partner," she clarified, realizing that in her embarrassment, she was rambling.

In no way was she prepared to hear him quietly tell her, "I am."

Cris stared at him, confused. "You are what—single or—?"

"Or," he told her. At the bewilderment in her eyes, he took pity on her and explained. "I was married for a while." He'd slipped a ring on Virginia's finger the moment he got out of the service. "My wife was killed in a car accident a little more than three years ago."

Sympathy flooded her and she ached for what Shane must have gone through.

"Oh, I'm so sorry," she murmured. As her soul reached out to his, she took his hand in hers, silently sealing the painful bond they now shared. "I didn't even know you were married. I lost touch with Nancy," she confessed, referring to his sister, who had been one of her two closest friends in high school.

"There's no reason for you to apologize," Shane said. Although he had to admit she did look appealing as she was doing so. "Things change, people move on." He shrugged. "That's life."

Nevertheless, she thought, she should have somehow sensed that someone as handsome and outgoing as Shane would easily have found someone to share his life with.

Wanting to change the focus of the conversation, Cris asked, "How is Nancy these days?"

Thinking of his younger sister, Shane smiled. "She lives up near San Francisco now. She's married, with twin boys and is working for some big design company. I'll let her know you asked about her," he promised. "She'll get a kick out of me doing some work for your family."

"Give her my love," Cris told him. *Okay, now you can leave,* she silently instructed herself. Yet she remained, as if glue had been applied to the soles of her shoes. She heard herself inviting him—again—to dinner. "So, despite my unfortunate foot-in-mouth moment, *will* you come to dinner tonight?"

He inclined his head. "I'd love to, but I hate to eat and run, and that's what I'd be doing if I had dinner here," he confessed. "I've got to be somewhere at seven."

He's got a date, you idiot, and he's trying to be nice about it by not waving it in your face. When will you ever be smart enough to take a hint? Not that you have any de-

signs on him, of course—but it certainly looks that way.

"Fair enough," she said with perhaps a touch too much cheerfulness. "You tell me what you'd like for dinner and I'll have it waiting for you by the time you come in to eat. Say at six?" she suggested, watching his expression for some sort of clue. "Or do you need to get going earlier? If you're really in a hurry, I can have it wrapped to take out," she volunteered.

That would be the easiest solution, but it had its drawbacks. "Tempting, but I'd just as soon eat here. If I brought the food with me, I wouldn't be able to divide it into enough pieces to share it equally."

She stared at him. That had to be the strangest comment she'd ever heard about eating one of her meals. What was he talking about?

"You've lost me," she told Shane honestly. "Are you feeding something?" It sounded as though he was working with pets or at least some kind of animal. "Because I can certainly give you more than just a regular portion to take with you—"

"Stop," he ordered before she continued

any further down the wrong path. "You're way too generous, Cris, but even an extra-large portion still wouldn't be enough."

Just *what* was he planning on feeding? "You realize you're making me incredibly curious."

As a rule, Cris didn't believe in prying— what people did was their own business. But Shane was scattering just enough tasty bread crumbs before a hungry woman to make her ravenous for more.

He grinned at her. "And yet, you're not asking questions," he marveled. She had always been an unusual person, Shane recalled with more than a touch of admiration.

"Well, if you wanted me to know, you'd tell me—although," Cris had to admit in all honesty, "I really do wish you would."

Again he laughed, intuiting what was likely going on in her mind.

"It's actually a lot less exciting than you're probably imagining," he told Cris. "I volunteer at a homeless shelter two, three evenings a week—more if I'm between jobs," he confided. "I fix things at the shelter that break down, do whatever heavy lifting might be needed—literally and otherwise," he tacked on before she could inquire. "In general, I pitch in wherever a body is needed. Kind of like 'a jack of all trades, master of none' thing," he finished.

She took exception to how Shane just naturally played himself down. "I have a feeling you're good at all," she told him honestly. An idea hit her. She knew she didn't have to run it past her father—or Alex, who were both very big on charity and doing their share. "I tell you what. Every night when I close down the kitchen, there's usually leftover good food that we don't use the next day—like the bread I bake and some of the extra portions of food. Once they've been served in the dining area, we're not allowed to put them back into our refrigerator to serve the next day. Why don't I set those items aside and on the days you go to the shelter, you can take them with you. Just give me a heads-up on the days you volunteer."

He considered her offer less than a moment. "Well, I pass by the shelter on my way home from here. I can drop off your donation every night if you're really serious."

She thought that an odd way for him to

word his acceptance. "Why wouldn't I be serious?" she wanted to know, puzzled.

"Sorry, just my basic wariness rising to the surface." He had to remember who he was dealing with. Cris had always struck him as one of the "good ones."

"I deal with a lot of people whose favorite phrase is 'the check's in the mail' when it isn't. I tend to forget that there are really honest, decent people like you and your family around."

That there were gave him hope, the will to continue in a world made suddenly and painfully empty three years ago. He was just now finding his way again, finding how to rebuild himself and be whole once more.

Shane also realized that he liked working at the inn, liked interacting with Cris and her entire family. He was getting a kick out of her son. He'd have to be careful not to allow that to influence him. If he wasn't alert, his feelings might unconsciously cause him to slow down so he could continue working in this atmosphere, soaking in these people's company.

The compliment he'd just paid Cris and her family caused Cris to blush. She sensed her cheeks growing warm. Which meant they were already turning pink.

There were moments when she would have killed for a darker complexion, she thought wistfully.

It was *really* time to retreat—before she started guiding in ships from the sea with her glowing cheeks. "Well, I'd better be getting back to the kitchen and start making dinner." She paused one last time, cocking her head. "You'll stop by?" she asked, realizing that the matter really hadn't been settled.

"I'd be a fool not to."

"Wouldn't want that," Cris declared, turning on her heel.

Cris heard Shane humming "What A Wonderful World" as he raised his mask again to cover his mouth and nose then lowered the goggles he'd had on when she'd walked into the work area.

Cris smiled without realizing it as she hurried back to the kitchen.

CRIS GLANCED AT her watch again. She'd lost count of how many times she had looked at it in the past half hour. Right now, it was a little past six o'clock and neither Stevi nor

Andy had ducked into the kitchen to tell her Shane was in the dining area.

Where was he?

If he planned on being at the homeless shelter at seven, that didn't leave him much time to eat and get there… That was when she realized she had no idea where this homeless shelter was located.

Also, as a volunteer, Shane didn't punch a time clock, she reminded herself. He could be a few minutes late getting there—if he ever got here first.

You're spending way too much time thinking about something you have no business thinking about, Cris upbraided herself.

But in a way, she knew why she was fixating on Shane. Seeing him after all these years reminded her of a far simpler time. A time when life, with all its promises, lay before her, fresh and new. A time before the scaly hand of death had twisted her heart from her chest. In short, a time when innocence still surrounded her and anything was possible because ugliness had not yet reared its head in her world.

And, she had to admit, when she saw Shane playing with Ricky, it also reminded her of what her life could have been like if Mike had returned from his tour of duty on his own power rather than lying in a coffin.

"That is the fifth time in the past few minutes I have heard you sigh," Jorge, her assistant, observed. "Is everything all right?" he wanted to know, concerned.

"I can't breathe," she told him, the less-than-truthful reason coming automatically to her lips. "Allergies," she added for good measure.

Jorge stopped stirring the giant pot of potatoes he'd already mashed, now warming to perfection, and reached beneath the white tunic he always wore while in the kitchen. He extracted a small rectangular package from his pocket and held it out to her.

"Here, have one," he urged. "I take two a day for my allergies. They say to take one, but that doesn't work for the whole day," he told her. When she made no effort to reach for the small, over-the-counter medication from him, Jorge held it closer to her. "C'mon, try it, Miss Cris," he coaxed.

Embarrassed because she'd lied, Cris shook her head, sinking a little deeper into her untruth. "No, I already took something.

Wouldn't want to mix the two medications, just in case."

"No, of course not," Jorge agreed, although his tone really didn't tell her whether he believed her or was just playing along so she could save face.

Just then, Andy, the youngest of the Roman sisters, burst into the kitchen. "Red alert," she cried. "Hunky contractor guy has just landed in the dining room."

Cris caught Jorge looking at her knowingly. "I think that your allergy medication has arrived," he told her just before he turned back to his work.

Maybe she should have sent a tray to Shane's work area, Cris thought. Too late now.

"He's an old friend," she protested to Jorge, not wanting the man to think that anything was going on between Shane and her. She'd dated once in the five years since Mike's death and had vowed never again.

Everyone at the inn had watched her one attempt at dating go down in flames when she'd started seeing a man who, it swiftly became evident, wasn't fit to polish the boots of Mike's shadow. In addition, he tried to isolate her from her family and felt she wasn't being strict enough with Ricky. That had been the last straw.

After that little fiasco, she'd promised herself she would never date again—and if by some wild chance she did, she wouldn't let *anyone* at the inn know, so when *that,* too, blew up on her, she wouldn't be the object of sympathetic looks and peppy comments that were meant to raise her morale but only succeeded in lowering it.

"An old friend," Jorge echoed, then nodded. "The best kind to have."

Cris frowned, reading between the lines. "Don't patronize me, Jorge."

He frowned at the unfamiliar word. "I do not know what that means, but I am fairly sure I am not doing what you asked me not to do," he told her. And then he became very, very serious. "Do not let one mishap make you close yourself off," he warned. "Breathe with your whole body and soul," he counseled, obviously building on the allergy excuse she'd given him to explain why she was sighing.

Cris's hands were flying as she chopped celery stalks into tiny pieces. The staccato noise went to double time as she told her assistant, "Tell you what. You take care of your body and soul, Jorge, and I'll take care of mine. Deal?"

"But of course," Jorge agreed. "I would never try to argue with you."

He wasn't agreeing at all, she thought. His ironic tone told her as much. But she knew that if she said something to him about it, Jorge would simply feign innocence and somehow turn the whole thing into an object lesson with her being its unwilling recipient.

She would just have to get used to people looking out for her and worrying about her, she told herself. Everyone at the inn was like family, whether they shared DNA or not.

"Why do you not take the cause of your allergies his dinner?" Jorge suggested, nodding at the tray she had prepared. "I will stay here and watch over the rest of the cooking for you."

His offer was sweet, but if she accepted, she would be attesting that this man was special, someone apart from the others she helped. She was in no way ready for that and in no way was she even remotely searching for it.

"I don't need you to watch over anything for me," she informed Jorge. "Because I'm not going anywhere."

"That much is true," he concurred far too readily. "Unless, of course, you wake up and see that spending your life without someone there beside you really is like not going anywhere," he told her pointedly. "It is not even really living."

"I'm beginning to think that working in the inn's kitchen is the wrong place for you, Jorge. You should be working in a Chinese restaurant, baking fortune cookies and stuffing them with your words of wisdom," she told him with a laugh.

She gazed at the man who had been her assistant off and on for the past year and a half. She knew he meant well. But at the same time, he was making things difficult for her.

"Look, I know you believe you're helping, but I've got to find my own way through things—without help. Okay?"

"I am just making sure you are able to

see the road ahead of you," he said. "A lot of people lose their way."

"I'll keep that in mind," she promised.

The next moment, she left the kitchen and took a peek into the dining room.

Shane was sitting at the table.

And Ricky was sitting on a booster seat right beside him.

CHAPTER FIVE

CARRYING A TRAY WITH the dinner she'd prepared for Shane, Cris made her way over to the table. She kept her eyes fixed on her son as she approached.

"Aren't you supposed to be with Grandpa right now?" she asked Ricky. Shifting her eyes, she looked apologetically at Shane as she set his dinner in front of him. "I'm really sorry about this. He usually knows better than to bother people."

"I'm sure he does," Shane responded with amusement. "Which is why he's not bothering me." He glanced in Ricky's direction. "We were just having a man-to-man talk about the holidays."

"Holidays?" Cris repeated, a little confused at the reference. Just what was Ricky bending Shane's ear about? "Thanksgiving?" she guessed since it *was* the next holiday to come up.

"No, Christmas!" Ricky corrected her with all the enthusiasm of a child looking forward to what he considered the absolutely *best* time of the year.

"Inside voice, Ricky. You know you're supposed to use your inside voice when you're inside," Cris reminded her son, glancing around to see if anyone in the dining area appeared annoyed at the high pitch her son's voice had reached.

At this hour, only half the tables were filled. The rest of the inn's guests would be by later, unless they were eating out. She was relieved to see that none of the guests there seemed to have taken note of the exuberant boy.

"Sorry, Mama," Ricky said, lowering his voice by two octaves.

That minor issue out of the way, Cris addressed the one that Ricky had brought up. "Okay, what about Christmas?"

Ricky instantly dove into his explanation. "He said—"

She needed to nip this in the bud. "It's Mr. McCallister, not 'he,' Ricky. You know better than that," Cris said, then tactfully suggested, "and why don't you let Mr. Mc-Callister speak for himself?"

Rather than become crestfallen because he had to be quiet, the boy grinned and said, "Sure," then turned to look at his hero. "Tell Mama what you said."

"Yes, please, by all means," Cris added, "'Tell Mama.'"

Shane grinned at the reference and something inside her stomach fluttered.

"Well, I hope I didn't tread on any toes," Shane prefaced before he went on to fill Ricky's mother in on what he and her son had talked about. "But I told Ricky that I liked the smell and appearance of a real Christmas tree."

Unable to contain himself any longer, Ricky all but crowed, "See, Mama? Him, too."

Cris sighed. "Mr. McCallister agrees with me, too," she said, rephrasing her son's words.

"He does?" Ricky asked, beaming like a starburst. "Then it's okay? We can get a real tree again?" He took her answer for granted, assuming that it would be positive.

Rather than argue with Ricky about

whether they would get a real tree to celebrate Christmas, she slanted a glance toward Shane. She supposed that he deserved some sort of an explanation.

"Putting up an artificial tree instead of a real one is more practical," Cris told him.

All the other years, they'd had a tall, real tree standing in the main room. But escalating costs was a practical consideration that had Alex and her father leaning toward the purchase of a tree that could be used over and over each year.

As Cris stated what she assumed was most likely Alex's position, she saw a dubious expression on Shane's face. Curiosity had her asking, "What?"

Shane debated saying nothing, but one glance at the hopeful look on the boy's face had him making up his mind. After all, she *had* asked. "It's just that my own feeling is that Christmas isn't supposed to be about being practical. It's about the magic of the season."

Cris pressed her lips together, really torn. A few years back, she would have readily sided with him. However, she'd done a lot of growing up in the intervening years and was forced to look at things from a more practical point of view, which meant it was far more practical to buy a tree that could be used over and over than to throw away money on one that could only be used once.

"I understand what you're saying," she began.

That was all Ricky needed. "So we can go looking for a real tree, Mama? 'Cause Sha—I mean Mr. McCallister said he'd help—and he said he'd even bring his truck so we could bring the Christmas tree home with us when we find one."

"Mr. McCallister has better things to do than play deliveryman with our Christmas tree," Cris patiently pointed out.

But before her son could digest the information and offer a rebuttal, Shane said, "No, actually, I don't. I'd kind of like coming along to pick out and bring back the Christmas tree." When Cris looked at him quizzically, he explained, "It's been a few years since I went Christmas tree shopping." He shrugged haplessly. "What with Nancy living up north and my brother stationed back east, there's really not much of a reason to put up a tree."

"How about your parents?" Cris asked automatically, then immediately regretted it when she saw Shane shake his head. She knew what he was going to say before he said it.

"They're both gone."

What he had left unspoken—and that she understood—was that since his wife wasn't around to share in the season, even to acknowledge the day, much less get caught up in the season for its own sake, seemed pointless.

Part of the magic of the season was having someone to share it with.

"We hafta get a real tree for Sha—I mean Mr. McCallister," Ricky insisted, stumbling over Shane's surname again.

Shane made an appeal on Ricky's behalf. "Can he call me Shane?" he asked, looking at her. "It would be a lot easier on him," he added with a grin, ruffling the boy's hair.

She supposed that if Shane didn't mind, she could bend the rule in this instance.

"I guess we can make an exception," Cris allowed. "As long as you remember that it *is* an exception," she told her son.

In response, Ricky enthusiastically nodded like one of those bobblehead figures some people attached to dashboards.

"An 'ception," Ricky echoed—or did his best to.

Shane eyed her. "And the tree?" he asked, knowing she had to be the one to rule on that in this case. "Real or not?"

Cris caught herself giving in with ease. "I suppose we can get a real one again." Most likely, she had a feeling, her father was just waiting to be persuaded. Alex was the one they would need to win over. "To be honest, I think everyone prefers a real one. It's just that Alex has been trying to be extra conscientious about the bottom line—"

He knew all about bottom lines, but these days, he was living exceptionally frugally because he saw no reason or need to spend money beyond getting the essentials.

"Well, since I'll be one of the ones to enjoy seeing a real Christmas tree, I'll be happy to contribute to its final cost."

"That won't be necessary," Cris quickly told him, vetoing the idea of his paying a single red cent toward the tree. As it was, he was charging them far less for handling the renovations and additional construction than the other contractors had quoted.

Slanting a glance toward her son, who looked ready to levitate from his seat at any second, she interjected, "But if you don't mind coming along and allowing us the use of your truck as well as giving us the benefit of your opinion, that would be greatly appreciated."

The grin had his eyes crinkling appealingly. "Consider it done," he readily agreed. "Just tell me the day and time you want this expedition to get under way and I'll be there with bells on."

Hearing that caused Ricky to cover his mouth with his hands to contain the fit of giggles that descended over him.

"What's so funny?" Shane asked the boy, certain he'd said nothing to earn this level of levity.

"You're gonna be wearing bells?" Ricky asked, still giggling at the image that description conjured in his young head.

"It's just an expression, honey," Cris told the little boy. "Shane won't really be wearing bells."

"How do you know?" Shane asked, deliberately playing the scene out for Ricky's benefit. "Maybe I *will* be wearing them."

He saw the boy looking at him with huge, stunned eyes that contained a sliver of amusement in them, as well. Obviously Ricky couldn't make up his mind whether his new hero was putting his mother on.

"Can I wear 'em,' too, Mama?" Ricky wanted to know. "The bells?"

"We'll see," she said. She found that answer far easier to deliver than a straightforward no, which might stir up an argument. She glanced at the watch on her wrist. "Right now, Mr. McCallis—Shane has to be leaving."

Both Ricky and Shane turned to her, puzzled—and then, like a man waking from a quick nap, Shane laughed at his momentary lapse.

"You're right. I do. Thanks for reminding me." He looked at Ricky. "I guess I was just having too much fun and leaving slipped my mind."

"Where do you gotta go?" Ricky wanted to know.

"Ricky, don't pry," she admonished, but not as firmly as she might have. Ricky, she had to admit, got his inherent curiosity from her.

"It's okay," Shane told her, then addressed the boy's question. "I'm going to a homeless shelter."

The answer seemed to horrify Ricky. "Are you homeless?" he cried. "'Cause if you are, my grandpa'll let you stay here for free." Dorothy had told him about how kind his grandfather had been to her when she'd first come to the inn. The next moment, Ricky's face lit up as he got an idea. "You can stay in my room with me. I'll let you have my bed and I've got a sleeping bag I can put on the floor for me."

Impressed with the impromptu generosity the boy displayed without any prodding from his mother, Shane smiled at him warmly.

"That's really very generous of you, Ricky, but I'm not staying at the homeless shelter. I just go there to help out."

Wheat-colored eyebrows knit as the boy tried to absorb every word he'd been told.

"Help out what?" Ricky asked.

"Ricky—" Cris said, her tone warning the boy not to continue on this path. Not everyone liked being interrogated by a five-year-old.

But clearly Shane didn't belong to that group. "I don't mind him asking questions," he told her, then faced Ricky. "That's how he learns. Right, Ricky?"

Ricky seemed thrilled to be championed in this manner. "Right!"

"To answer your question, Ricky, I go there to help out any way I can. The people staying at the shelter aren't as lucky as you and I and your mom are."

Ricky appeared to take every word to heart. "We can give them our Christmas tree," he told Shane.

Shane laughed softly at the offer, putting his hand on the boy's shoulder. "I believe this comes under the heading of giving them the shirt off your back," he quipped, directing his comment to Cris.

The expression on Shane's face made her feel, just for an isolated second, as though they were actually sharing a moment. The very thought stirred a warmth within her as unexpected as it was comforting.

Meanwhile, Cris noticed that her son was glancing from her to Shane, as if doing his very best to understand what had just been said.

"I gotta give them my shirt?"

Even as he asked, Ricky tugged the bottom of his pullover out of the waistband of his pants. In another minute, he would have the shirt up, over his head and off his small body, fully intending to surrender it to Shane so he could do what he needed to with it. All Ricky knew was that he wanted to help Shane.

Laughing, Shane quickly stilled the little boy's fast-moving hands.

"No, stop," he said to Ricky. "I didn't mean you had to take off your shirt. It's just another way of saying you were being very giving."

"Oh," Ricky said, struggling to look as though he understood what was being said. Cris had a feeling that the boy didn't but was unwilling to let on in case his new hero would find him lacking in some way. "But you don't really want me to give my shirt to you?"

"Not today," Shane assured him with affection as he patted the boy's shoulder. And then he looked at Cris. "I'd better be going,"

Shane said again, attempting to come to terms with the sudden reluctance he was experiencing.

Was he just reluctant to leave, or was he reluctant to leave *her?*

He really wasn't sure.

Maybe it would be better if he didn't explore what might lie beneath that question, at least not yet. Right now, his life was relatively uncomplicated. Lonely, but uncomplicated. And he wanted to take some time deciding exactly what complications he would welcome into it and be equipped to handle. Not to mention what complications might just trip him up and take him in a direction he wasn't, as yet, prepared to go.

Even so, as he rose, Shane couldn't help thinking that staying here, talking to Cris and enjoying the unfiltered responses of her son, was really not a bad way to spend the rest of his evening.

You've got people waiting for you and responsibilities to meet, remember? Shane reminded himself.

He really had to get going. Shane nodded at his cleared plate. "Thanks for the meal.

I intend to pay you back in trade since you won't let me pay you for the food."

"You already *have* paid me back," Cris insisted, adding, "just by putting up with certain people." She deliberately kept her statement vague since Ricky was right there, absorbing every word between Shane and her.

"No 'putting up' involved," Shane assured her, indicating her son with his eyes. "I enjoyed every second of it."

He sounded sincere, but that could just be because she was hearing something that appealed to her. There was reality and then there was the reality she *wished* she had. This might well be the latter.

"I find that difficult to believe," she told Shane.

Cris recalled the one person she had dated in the past five years. The man had made it clear after a couple of dates that he didn't regard her as a package deal, meaning that he didn't want to interact with her son if there was any way he could avoid it.

She had sent him packing that same day.

Shane's dark blue eyes met hers and she saw that he was completely serious as he told her, "Don't." She assumed he was telling her that she shouldn't be having any difficulty in believing he liked dealing with Ricky and putting up with the boy's somewhat demanding personality.

Shane McCallister won a place in her heart that very moment.

It took her a second to realize that Ricky was trying to get her attention. After a beat, she looked at him and he asked, "Can I go with him, Mama?"

Getting the boy to speak properly felt like a never-ending battle. "May I go with him," Cris corrected him patiently.

The lesson was lost on Ricky. He took her words at face value.

"You wanna go, too? Then we can both go, right?" Ricky asked eagerly, swinging his little feet beneath the table. Any faster and Cris was certain he'd take off like a miniature helicopter.

"No, Ricky, I was just trying to correct your grammar. And no, you can't go with Shane. You have homework to do and I've got more dinners to serve, so we're both grounded."

Out of the corner of her eye, she saw

Shane pause at the dining area's threshold, turn around and wave to her and Ricky. She waved back, as did her son.

Cris stood there, firmly telling herself that her stomach *hadn't* just leaped up in response, that if anything, it was only reacting to something she'd eaten earlier in the day.

But she knew she was making excuses. Poor ones, at that. They certainly weren't convincing her of anything other than the fact that Shane's proximity created mini tidal waves in her stomach.

Cris forced herself to focus on the immediate situation: she needed Ricky escorted back to his grandfather.

Glancing at the boy, she had a feeling that if she sent him off on his own the way she normally did, he would probably race after Shane and attempt to talk his way into going to the shelter with him. Most likely he'd tell Shane he had her blessings.

So, grasping his hand firmly in hers, Cris waved and managed to catch Stevi's attention as she finished jotting down an order.

When Stevi crossed to her, Cris told her sister, "Take him to Dad. Ricky's got some homework to do before he's a free man tonight."

"Okay. Trade," Stevi bargained, handing over the old-fashioned order pad she had in her hand. "That's from Ms. Carlyle," she said, referring to their one permanent resident, Anne Carlyle, a retired elementary school teacher who had been coming to the inn since before their father had taken over managing it from *his* father, Kent Roman.

This was a trade that she could readily live with, Cris thought.

"Deal," she declared, and handed off her son to her sister.

CHAPTER SIX

RICHARD ROMAN LET the swinging door into the kitchen close behind him. "A penny for your thoughts," he said to the only other occupant in the room.

The dinner rush was over and cleanup already done. Jorge had left the premises.

His daughter was standing in front of the industrial range, for once *not* a vision of perpetual motion. Her mind was definitely elsewhere.

It wasn't like her.

Cris startled and turned away from the range to look at her father.

She offered him a bright, affectionate smile as she played back his words in her head. "Sorry, Dad, a penny doesn't buy anything these days."

Richard laughed softly—and just possibly with a bit of nostalgia. "Don't I know it."

He paused for a moment, then drew a step closer, his eyes intent on hers.

His fatherly intuition, which had taken time for him to cultivate, told him that something was off. He even had a gut feeling he knew what that "something" was. But for now, he kept that to himself. Things always worked out better if Cris was the one who volunteered the information.

"Anything wrong?" he asked in a voice that was infinitely sympathetic.

She shook her head a little too quickly, a little too casually. "No, I'm just thinking."

His eyes continued to hold hers. "About?"

She shrugged. "Nothing that's worth taking up your time," she told him. This wasn't a topic that was easily discussed—or even understood. She needed to work it out in her own head first before attempting to say anything to her father or anyone else in the family.

"Why don't you let me be the judge of that?" he replied. "And for the record, everything that concerns you and your sisters is worth taking up my time," he reminded her. "Just because none of you need me to braid your hair or drive you off to the mall anymore doesn't mean I'm bowing out of your lives or stepping away from the father business." He patted her cheek affectionately. "Face it, Cris. You're stuck with me. I'm going to be your dad until they lay me to rest beside your mother."

"Which is not going to be for a long, long time," Cris insisted with feeling. She knew her sisters still thought of their father as a dad. And he was the invisible glue that held the family all together.

"Absolutely," Richard agreed. Then his playful tone receded. "Is it the wedding?" he asked kindly, voicing what he had intuited.

He knew that despite their occasional flare-ups, his daughters loved one another fiercely, that they would defend one another with their last breath and that no significant jealousy flowed between them.

But he was also sensitive to the undercurrents in their relationships in certain situations. While he knew that Cris was more than happy for Alex because her older sister was marrying Wyatt, he also felt the impending marriage had to stir up memories for Cris. Both the good ones *and* the bad.

When Cris had married Mike, the vows

they had exchanged had included the phrase "till death do us part." No one had expected death to enter the equation for decades to come.

But it had.

As had his Amy, whom Richard felt had been taken from him far too soon, Mike had been forced to break his vow with Cris. "Forever" had turned out to be finite.

Unlike Amy, Mike had not been buried in the family cemetery. His wealthy, upper-crust parents had insisted that Mike be laid to rest in the mausoleum where the rest of his family for generations back was buried. Out of respect for their wishes, Cris hadn't contested the matter. But Richard knew that his daughter missed being able to visit Mike's grave whenever she wanted to, the way he did with his Amy.

"No, it has nothing to do with the wedding," Cris assured him. "Really, I was just taking a little mental break from everything, that's all."

She uttered the words as convincingly as she could. Cris didn't want her father to suspect what she'd really been thinking about: Shane and coming to terms with what she admitted in the privacy of her own heart was a mysteriously unsettling attraction to him.

Feeling such an attraction somehow seemed disloyal to her. Disloyal to Mike's memory. Yes, Mike was gone and had been for five very long years, but she had expected to go to her grave loving only him. Her one short-lived venture into the world of dating had reinforced that reality for her.

Rising onto her toes, she brushed her lips against her father's cheek.

"Really, Dad, you worry much too much. You need to stop thinking about us all the time and get in a little socializing while you're still young enough to really enjoy it."

"I'm doing just fine and don't go trying to change the subject on me." He laughed. "I'm on to you, Christina Roman MacDonald."

"I don't know what you mean," she told him. "Honestly. I didn't know there was a subject."

"Actually, there is," he confessed, remembering the conversation he'd had with Ricky that had sent him looking for her earlier. "What's this I hear about a mini-expedition to find a real Christmas tree for the inn's main room?"

Well, there certainly were no secrets around here, not even for a few hours, Cris couldn't help thinking. She wondered if her son had told her father about the change in plans the second that the little boy had run into the room.

"I take it Ricky's been bending your ear."

Her father laughed. That was putting it mildly. They all knew how the boy could talk nonstop for what seemed like hours on end.

"Ricky has been talking about nothing else *but* that for the past hour," her father told her. "I finally had to turn him over to Andy to get him ready for bed. That boy's got too much energy for me—my ears are still ringing."

"You've got to save that energy for the ladies, Dad," she said with a wink.

"I don't intend for there to be any 'ladies,' Cris," Richard reminded his daughter firmly.

Cris crossed her arms before her as she leaned back against the cold stove. "Rosemary will be very disappointed to hear you say that."

Richard blinked. "Rosemary?"

Boy, talk about being in denial, she thought. How could he miss all the signs? "Rosemary Cambridge. Our neighbor. The lady who comes in to occasionally lend me a hand whenever you or Alex manage to book a mini-convention at the inn."

"I know who she is," Richard answered with just a trace of impatience. "What I don't know is where you got this completely strange idea that Rosemary would have any feelings one way or the other about my socializing—or not socializing."

"Dad, *look* at the lady sometime," Cris declared. "If that woman were any more taken with you, her eyes would have little hearts in them like those characters in those vintage cartoon shows you like to watch with Ricky."

Richard shook his head, dismissing her observations. "You've been standing over pots of boiling water for far too long, Cris. The vapors have infiltrated your brain."

"I'm not the only one who's noticed the way Rosemary looks at you, Dad, and the others aren't anywhere *near* pots of boiling water. Face it, you have a fan."

Richard waved a hand at her, signaling

an end to the discussion. "The subject was Christmas trees," he reminded her. "Ricky told me that he, you and our general contractor were going to go hunting for 'the perfect Christmas tree.'" He looked at Cris intently. "Are you?"

She didn't want her father to think she'd put the boy up to it, was using Ricky as a shill for something that she wanted. That wasn't how she did things and she was fairly certain her father knew it.

But just in case he'd forgotten, she said, "He's just talking, Dad. Seems he told Shane he wanted us to get a real tree and Shane told *him* that he liked real trees, too, but—"

Richard cut short her explanation. "So do I."

Cris stared at him, bemused. "I thought you said a real one wasn't practical."

"No, *Alex* said a real one wasn't practical," he corrected. "Alex likes real trees, also. She's just looking to save the inn money in the long run," he told Cris. "As far as I'm concerned, that isn't the way to do it. We'll find other ways to economize if it comes down to that again. For the time being," he continued, never fond of making predictions that went too far into the future, "things are going well.

"So you, my overly bouncy grandson and that contractor friend of yours can feel free to bring back a really nice specimen. You can start the hunt right after Thanksgiving is behind us," he added.

That was when they normally went tree shopping. "In other words, business as usual," Cris said.

Richard smiled at that. "Those words have a nice ring." He made to leave the kitchen but paused for a moment longer. "You're sure there's nothing you want to talk about?" he queried, just in case.

"I'm sure Ricky talks enough for all of us, Dad," she answered evasively. "In my opinion, what you need is a little me-time."

"Later," he said, dismissing the notion. He liked filling his days with family, not deliberately emptying them. "As for now, two ears, no waiting."

As she regarded her father, Cris thought he was looking at her as if he expected her to tell him that there *was* something she needed to get off her chest or just talk through.

"And very nice ears they are, too," she replied glibly. "Now get out of my kitchen—" she pointed toward the swinging door "—so that I can close down. Go be Dad to Alex— have that birds-and-bees talk with her you never got around to," she advised with a wink.

Richard tried to bank a sudden wave of anxiety. "You don't mean—"

Cris laughed. She hadn't meant to get him flustered. "No, Dad, I *don't* mean—Alex is fine. We're all fine," she assured him. "Put your feet up and take a Dad-break. The night's clear and crisp. Sit outside and ab- sorb some of that fresh air."

He tried to extract a promise from her to appease his conscience. "And you'll talk to me if something's on your mind or bother- ing you?"

"You have my word," Cris said, holding up her right hand as if taking a solemn vow. "You will be the first person I run to if I'm suddenly having a crisis or an anxiety at- tack—or bursting with a secret," she added. "Good enough?"

He inclined his head. "I guess it'll have to be."

As Richard turned to leave, he recalled

something he needed to share with his second born. "Oh, I almost forgot. Alex asked me to give you this when I saw you."

Cris eyed her father curiously, but there was no need to ask what "this" referred to since he was holding out an envelope to her.

As she took it from him, Cris had only to glance at the front of the envelope to realize who it was from. She recognized the handwriting and because she did, she could feel something suddenly stiffening inside her. Involuntarily, she braced herself, although she couldn't have really said for what.

Richard saw the change immediately. "Cris?" her father said in response to the fearful look that came over her face. "What is it?"

"Most likely nothing," she replied even as she felt her breath growing short and had the ominous feeling that she was about to read something that would upset her in some way.

Richard wasn't about to stand on ceremony and wait for her to tell him—or not tell him—as she saw fit. Cris was his daughter, and if something had frightened her, he deserved to know so that he could protect her emotionally—and physically if need be.

"Who's it from?" he asked, since she obviously knew who'd sent the envelope, despite the absence of a return address or even the sender's name scribbled in the corner.

"Mike's mother." The words felt like dry cotton in her mouth. They stuck to every corner, making her gag.

The relationship between her and Mike's parents was polite, but strained at best. The few times she'd been in their company—they'd visited their grandson on several occasions—she'd felt uncomfortable. Though they'd never said it to her in so many words, she knew that in their eyes, she didn't measure up to the kind of woman they felt their son should have married. Mike used to tell her they had all the warmth and flexibility of stalagmites.

Ignoring the fluttering butterflies in her stomach and taking a breath to prepare herself for whatever she discovered inside the envelope, she opened the envelope and extracted the single folded sheet of paper inside.

It read almost like a business letter—short and to the point.

For her father's benefit, she read it out loud.

"Dear Christina,
My husband and I are coming down to San Diego the first week of December to see you and our grandson. It's time we had a serious conversation about his future.
Sincerely yours,
Marion MacDonald."

Cris pressed her lips together as she carefully refolded the letter and slipped it back into the envelope. The fluttering butterflies in her stomach had turned into Boeing 747s.

Raising her eyes to her father, she did her best to still the queasiness that threatened to overtake her. "What do you think she means by that?"

"Maybe they just miss seeing Ricky," her father suggested kindly, "and she's saying they want to adopt a more hands-on approach to Ricky's future." He offered her an encouraging smile. "After all, he's a lovable kid—a lot like his mother," he added kindly.

"Maybe you're right," Cris agreed, doing her best not to allow her fear to seep into her voice.

"You don't think so, do you?" Richard asked gently.

"Do you?"

He had always been honest with his daughters. Now was no different. "Frankly, I'm not sure what to think. Maybe Marion and Arthur feel guilty they haven't taken a more active part in Ricky's life. Mike's death had to have hit them hard. He was their only son," he reminded Cris.

"Then they should have been nicer to him when he was alive," Cris cried, her emotions getting the better of her. She remembered the stories Mike had told her when she finally got him to talk to her about his childhood. He'd always felt that nothing he did was good enough, that all his parents cared about was the family image, so eventually he just stopped trying to measure up to their standards and went his own way. But she knew that their disappointment in him had hurt him, even though he'd never said it in so many words.

"Maybe they regret the past and have come around. The only way they know how to make up for it is to take more of an interest in their grandson," her father proposed.

They would have been hard-pressed to take *less* of an interest in Ricky, she thought. And that had certainly not been her fault. "I did my part. I tried to maintain ties, Dad, I really did," she told him. She'd deliberately turned a blind eye to their tacit disapproval of her. "I sent them pictures of Ricky, I remembered their birthdays and sent cards for all the holidays. I kept them abreast of Ricky's progress from being a three-pound premature infant with less-than-good odds to survive to his being the darling chatterbox he is today. And they sent back cards with their names printed on the inside, like some corporation, along with checks. A few personal words instead of checks would have been more appreciated," she told her father.

"Maybe they don't know how to reach out and that's why they're coming down to talk with you. Maybe they're hoping to make a new start," Richard said kindly.

"Maybe," she echoed. But she couldn't shake the nervous feeling that had taken hold of her. "You see only the good in people, don't you, Dad?"

"Well, if you go the route of seeing just

the good," he told her simply, "you'd be surprised how many people live up to that."

She held up an index finger, making a point. "Yes, but those people have souls. I'm not so sure that's the case with Mike's parents." Although she'd gone through the motions of maintaining ties with the Mac-Donalds because they were Ricky's grandparents, in her heart she'd never forgiven them for being so distant with their own son. Mike had deserved better.

She pulled in a bracing breath. "You remember that thing I said earlier about letting you know if I'm having a crisis or an anxiety attack? Well, this might just be your lucky night, Dad, because I think I'm having both."

"Everything will work itself out, Cris," he assured her. "And I'm not just giving them a pass, honey. I'm saying that some people change for the better. Think positive until you find out otherwise." He took both her hands in his again, trying to impress this on her. "If you think negative and things do work out, you will have wasted all that time and effort by anticipating the worst."

She had another thought about that. "And if the worst does happen?"

"Anticipating it has no benefit," he stated. "Better to be hopeful than not."

Her father really believed that, she thought. But she herself no longer felt that way. Yet she didn't want to make waves. It was bad enough that as the inn's host, her father would have to deal with two humorless former in-laws.

"I'll do my best, Dad."

"Can't ask for more," he told her with a wide smile. "Now, until these people actually get here, I want you to put them out of your mind. Don't try to second-guess what they want. We'll find out when the time comes. Right now, we all want and *need* you to be happy."

She laughed. There was that wonderful support again, popping up when she needed it the most. "God knows, we all need you. Especially me."

He squeezed her hand. "Always here for you, Cris. Always here for you."

Her eyes crinkled as she smiled at him. "I know that, Dad."

And the best part of it was, she did.

CHAPTER SEVEN

CRIS HELD HER breath as she eased the door open, careful not to make a sound. Having finally closed the kitchen for the night, she had come upstairs to look in on her son and make sure he was asleep.

Rather than a night-light, which he claimed created "spooky shadows" on the walls, Ricky slept with the lamp on his nightstand turned down low.

She smiled to herself as she tiptoed into his bedroom. He was asleep now—after running around all day, how he wouldn't have collapsed out of sheer exhaustion was hard to see. Cris had to resist the temptation to tuck the blanket around him a little more. Ricky's much dragged around, much beloved stuffed animal, a mutt affectionately named Floppy for his big, floppy, cocker spaniel ears, was tucked into bed beside him.

This was an image that she stored away in the recesses of her mind. Someday, she thought, when her son was all grown-up and off on his own, she would pull out this image and remember what it was like to have him still and close to her.

What if Mike's parents want to take him away?

The terrifying idea came out of nowhere. With almost superhuman effort, she banished it, telling herself she was letting her imagination run away with her. Mike's parents weren't young anymore. Why would they want to raise a five-year-old?

The answer was they wouldn't, she silently insisted. Her father was right. She'd make herself crazy if she overthought this.

There was nothing to be afraid of, she maintained fiercely.

"I love you, little man," Cris whispered, her heart overflowing as she gazed down at her son.

Ricky stirred, obviously not as deeply asleep as she'd assumed.

"I love you, too, Mama," he responded, although his eyes remained shut. In another moment, he was back in the arms of Morpheus, the Greek god of sleep.

That was close, she acknowledged.

Taking care not to make any noise, Cris backed out of the room, then eased the door shut again. When she turned away, she came within inches of bumping into Alex. Only the greatest self-control had her swallowing the cry of surprise that instantly rose to her lips.

Her hand on her chest as if to physically still her pounding heart, Cris looked up at her older sister. "Are you trying to give me a heart attack?"

Their father had just told Alex who Cris's letter was from and she had immediately gone searching for her sister, hoping against hope that the news hadn't been upsetting.

"No, I'm trying to give you an apology," Alex told her truthfully. "If I'd known that letter was from the Wicked Witch of the West and her cohort, I wouldn't have handed it to Dad to pass on to you."

At times Alex acted even more protective than their father. "Withholding mail is a punishable offense, Alex," Cris said wryly.

"So is murder," Alex told her, threading

her arm through hers. "But I'm seriously contemplating it." There wasn't a hint of a smile on her face or humor in her voice. "Taking out that woman permanently before she gets here could only improve society."

"We don't know why she's coming yet," Cris pointed out, doing her best to be fair for Mike's sake even though she could feel those giant butterflies in her stomach again. "After all they *are* Mike's parents. Maybe Dad's right. Maybe they've recognized the error of their ways and just want to mend fences, let the past be the past."

Alex withdrew her arm and stared at her. "You can't *possibly* believe that, can you?" she asked, incredulous. "Cris, Mike *eloped* with you so he wouldn't have to find an excuse not to invite them to his wedding. That alone should tell you something."

The tumult in her abdomen increased. It was all she could do not to put her hand over her stomach to hold it down. "They *are* Ricky's grandparents."

Alex snorted. "I don't care. I don't trust them."

Cris knew exactly what Alex was saying and a large part of her agreed with her older sister. But she couldn't indulge herself. She had to be the bigger person, see the bigger picture.

"Maybe they've come to their senses and regret not being more a part of Ricky's life." Oh, God, she hoped that didn't mean they were thinking of moving down here to be closer to him. Maybe it was selfish of her, but the prospect of seeing the barely veiled disapproval in their eyes, looking at her on a regular basis, made her feel even more nauseous.

"Did they say so in the letter?" Alex asked. Her tone indicated that she already knew the answer to that question.

Cris shrugged helplessly. "Well, not in so many words…"

"How about in *any* words?" Alex challenged, her eyes intent on her sister's.

"She said they wanted to discuss Ricky's future with me," Cris replied quietly. "Dad said I shouldn't worry and think the worst until it happens."

Alex slowly urged her sister toward the stairs. "Dad is a lovely, kind man who's giving you advice straight out of a 1950's sitcom. His philosophy belongs to a kinder, gentler time," Alex told her. "Unfortunately, the very wealthy, less than warm-and-toasty Mr. and Mrs. MacDonald do not. If they were my ex in-laws—"

"Former in-laws," Cris corrected. "I didn't divorce Mike," she said, an incredible sadness echoing in her voice. "I lost him."

"Okay, former in-laws," Alex conceded. "If they were *my* former in-laws, I'd summarily tell them to get lost the next time I caught either one of them looking disapprovingly at me."

If only things were that simple, Cris thought, wishing with her whole heart that they were. But she had Ricky to consider. "I can't do that."

"Well, I can," Alex told her. The next moment, she was volunteering for the mission, almost begging for a chance to go through with it. "And I will. Just say the word, Cris. *Please* say the word."

"No, you won't," Cris told her firmly. "I'll hear her—them—out," she corrected herself. Because Marion MacDonald tended to take over any room she was in, at times it was hard to remember that she was only one half of the duo. Cris had no doubts that the woman also tended to forget she was married. She made the decisions in the union and was clearly the stronger-willed one.

"Okay, you hear them out—and *then* can I kill them?" Alex wanted to know.

This time Cris laughed. Alex had succeeded in making her feel better. "No, you can't."

Alex gazed at her sharply, as if trying to analyze what lay beneath the protest. "Don't tell me you *like* them," she pleaded. At times Cris, like their father, was just too kindhearted, willing to forgive people and allow them a second chance whether they deserved it or not. In Alex's opinion, Mike's parents didn't.

"No," Cris said honestly, "but I like you and I wouldn't want to see you in jail for killing Ricky's grandparents."

"We'll play it by ear but I'm not making any promises about completely abandoning murder as a last resort," Alex told her. When Cris gave her a look, Alex added, "It's the best I can do. For now," she said, changing the subject as she glanced at her watch, "feel like taking in a late movie?"

"Only if it's on television," Cris answered.

Exhaustion was finally catching up with her and she didn't feel up to going out. "I'm feeling pretty drained," she apologized.

Alex was nothing if not flexible. "Okay, new plan. Why don't we sit out on the veranda, just two single women, and talk about anything that comes to mind? My single-woman days are numbered," she reminded Cris, in case her sister was going to turn this suggestion down as well, "and I'd like to make the most of what I have left. Humor me," she requested, hoping that was enough to forestall Cris from begging off.

Cris shook her head, quietly marveling at the almost seamless way Alex could always maneuver things to get the outcome she wanted.

"You realize that you make it hard to refuse," Cris accused.

Alex laughed. "That's the whole idea," she told her. "So, how about it? Up to a little serious veranda sitting?"

Being with Alex or one of her other sisters was far preferable to being alone with her thoughts right now, Cris knew. No matter how much she didn't want to think about any problems and complications that might be just ahead with this visit from her former in-laws, she knew if she called it a night and went off to her room, that was exactly what would happen. Dark thoughts would fester in her mind and keep her awake, guaranteeing that tomorrow would turn into a disaster when she showed up for work emulating one of those zombie creatures that seemed so popular these days.

"Okay, why not?" she finally conceded.

"Wow, if you were any more enthusiastic, you might make me feel drunk with power," Alex cracked.

Alex didn't have a lock on sarcasm, Cris decided. "Sorry, left my cheerleading pompoms in my other locker," she said.

"Right next to your cheerful personality, I see," Alex observed, determined to have the last word.

Cris headed down the stairs. Maybe Alex was right, and she was being far too somber. She was blowing the letter out of proportion. Everything would be all right, she told herself. It *had* to.

"Sorry," she apologized, "it's been a long day."

"Apology accepted," Alex replied.

Once they reached the first floor, they went out the back way to the wraparound veranda. The first hint of fall made the air nippy, and none of the inn's guests were outside, taking in the night air. Consequently, Cris and her sister had their choice of seats.

Cris opted for the first chair she came to and dropped wearily into it. Alex took the one right next to hers. For a moment, there was nothing but the sound of crickets looking for each other and a little love in the dark.

Then Alex broke the silence. "I hear we're having a real Christmas tree again."

Expecting to be berated, Cris said defensively, "Actually, that wasn't my fault."

"Who said it was a fault?" Alex asked innocently. "I didn't say I thought someone was to blame. To be honest, I'm glad I was overruled," she confided. "I was just trying to be frugal. But I like real trees as much as anyone in this family," she went on, defending herself. "And when you come right down to it," she continued thoughtfully, "I guess having a real tree is in keeping with the inn's motif." She grinned as she rolled the thought over in her head. "I doubt very much if they had artificial Christmas trees when Ruth Roman turned her home into a bed-and-breakfast. Was it Ricky who championed the choice?"

Cris nodded. "But he had help."

"Yeah—" Alex laughed "—his mom."

"No, actually, it was the contractor you hired," Cris said, having done her best to word the statement so that there was just polite, formal distance between Shane and her.

Whether by design or accident, Alex didn't pick up on that distance. Instead, she pointed out one of the reasons the general contractor had been hired to begin with. "The one you knew."

Cris surrendered. There was percentage in fighting the obvious. "Yeah, the one I knew," she acknowledged. "Shane agreed with Ricky about the tree, which was all Ricky needed. The whole thing escalated from there and—"

"So tell me about this contractor who likes live Christmas trees," Alex urged, leaning in even closer to her.

Cris blinked and stared at her. "What do you mean, 'tell you' about him? You see him every day and you interact with him.

You're the one who has more contact with him, telling him what you want done around the inn."

Alex gave her a penetrating look. "I wasn't asking about the obvious, Cris."

"Okay, I'll bite," Cris declared, surrendering for a second time. She tucked her feet under her on the chair and wrapped her arms around her knees, forming a tight little ball. "What *were* you asking about?"

Giving Cris the once-over, Alex frowned. "Well, for one thing, why are you suddenly pulling your body into yourself like that? I swear, if you were a turtle, by now you would have disappeared completely into your shell. What gives?" Alex wasn't trying to drive Cris off; rather, she was trying to bring her out—unsuccessfully at the moment.

"It's chilly," Cris said defensively.

"And the questions are making things too warm for you?" Alex asked knowingly.

She hated it when Alex was right and she didn't want her to be. Cris sniffed. "I don't understand what you're talking about."

They were going around and around on this. Alex was prepared to remain there all night until she got Cris to admit to at least liking this Shane person.

"What I'm talking about is that you seem to like this guy."

Cris supposed there was no harm in admitting to that—as long as she kept the admission light. "Well, he's a nice man."

"Nobody said he wasn't," Alex indicated.

"But I don't 'like' like him." Cris was quick to disclaim what Alex clearly believed before the discussion got out of hand. "Not the way you're implying," she insisted.

Alex was *not* about to buy what Cris was selling. "Hey, Cris, there's nothing wrong in letting yourself like someone again. Mike wouldn't have expected you to become a nun. He would have wanted you to pick yourself up and go on with your life."

Cris hadn't lain on her bed, sobbing her heart out every morning, noon and night—even though she'd wanted to in the beginning. That should have been enough for her family.

"I *am* going on with my life," Cris insisted.

But Alex shook her head. "Correction— you are putting one foot in front of the other, getting up every morning and following a routine." She had to see the difference, Alex thought, didn't she? "You're there for Ricky, there for the inn, there for the family—"

"That's what I just said," Cris declared. "I'm going on with my life."

Alex carried on as if she hadn't been interrupted. "But you're not 'there' for yourself. You're not letting yourself *feel,* Cris," she persisted, stressing the word.

Okay, enough of being polite, of letting others think they knew how to conduct her life better than she did. "What I'm not letting myself do, Alex, is set myself up for another fall," she said vehemently. "It hurts like you wouldn't believe. Falling from the sky without a parachute would be easier in comparison." Now that she'd started talking, she found she couldn't stop. It was as if she had to purge everything from her system.

"If I close my eyes, I can still see that marine and that chaplain, walking up the walk, standing there in the doorway, telling me how very sorry they were to be the ones to bring the news that Mike was coming home early, but not the way either one of us dreamed he would."

Was Cris afraid that Shane would suddenly enlist and wind up leaving her the way Mike had left her? "From what I hear," Alex said, "Shane already served time, and left with an honorable discharge."

That made no difference, Cris thought. Scars were scars.

"Lots of ways to be hurt, Alex," she finally said quietly.

Alex was not about to give up. "One of which is hiding from the world."

Cris drew herself up. "I am *not* hiding, I'm just affording the world a wide path." She blew out a breath, more than tired. "Alex, I didn't agree to come out here with you to be lectured."

"I'm not lecturing," Alex protested with feeling.

"Okay," Cris augmented, "I didn't agree to come here with you to be nagged."

That word, Cris knew, was one with which Alex took particular umbrage. "I'm not doing that, either," she said.

Cris shifted in the wicker chair and faced her sister. "Alex, you're my older sister and I love you with my whole heart, but trust me on this—you nag."

Alex raised her chin defensively. "I don't nag—I repeat," she corrected.

Cris laughed. That was one way to put it, she thought. "Yes, you do. You repeat—over and over and over." Before Alex could say anything further to defend herself or explain the rationale behind her actions, Cris held up her hand and loudly announced, "New topic."

Well, if Cris had something else to get off her chest, she was game to listen. "Go ahead," Alex urged.

Shifting in her seat, Cris asked, "How many guests have you booked into the inn for Thanksgiving?"

"Why?" The question was reflexive—as was the answer. "Is that when the piranha and her husband are descending on us?"

"No, Marion's letter said they were coming sometime in December," Cris said automatically, then banished the thought, as well as the woman and her husband, from her mind. She knew that there was no way she could function otherwise. The worry would paralyze her. "I'm just trying to get a handle on how many turkeys I need to order."

Alex supposed it was never too early to

plan. There she and Cris were always in agreement.

"Well, right now," Alex told her, "we've got fifteen guests staying at the inn during that time. I'd count on at least a few more than that since the inn always gets some last-minute stragglers, as well."

Cris nodded. "And there're seven of us— Wyatt'll be here, right?" It was a rhetorical question, since he'd always been part of the family, one way or another.

"He'll be here," Alex confirmed, "but don't you mean there'll be eight of us?"

Cris jumped to the only conclusion that seemed logical to her. "Wyatt's bringing a friend?"

Was Cris really that thick—or was she just playing coy? Neither option seemed like the answer from where she was sitting.

"No, but you are." When Cris looked at her quizzically, Alex spelled it out for her. "Shane's coming."

Cris waved away her statement. "He'll be with his family."

But Alex, with her finger eternally on the pulse of practically everything, knew better.

"His sister is up north and his brother's

back east—and Shane's working on the inn, which he promised to have done by the first of the year, so he'll be here, not up the coast *or* back east. I thought that since he's being so conscientious and, by the way, doing a really terrific job, the least we can do is have him over for Thanksgiving—" She peered at Cris. "Unless, of course, you have some objections."

"No," Cris replied, staring up at the night sky to deliberately avoid Alex's probing eyes, "I have no objections."

She thought she heard Alex murmur "Good," but she wasn't sure and she certainly wasn't about to ask. Instead, Cris simply savored the momentary respite from her take-charge sister. She had a feeling that respites would be few and far between in the coming days.

Very far between.

CHAPTER EIGHT

"WHAT DO YOU mean you haven't picked out your wedding dress yet?" Stevi demanded, appalled as she followed Alex into the kitchen.

The timbre of her voice was so jarring that Cris, clearing away the remnants of the late lunch, almost dropped the tray she was holding.

Her younger sister's tone, Cris thought, was far more suited to that of a wild-eyed prophet foretelling the end of the world, a date six days away and set in stone.

Alex, for a change, looked completely un-fazed, as cool and laid-back as Stevi was not. "I've got time, Stevi, don't have a coronary."

"No, you do *not* have time," Stevi cried. She stretched her legs so as to get in front of Alex as well as in her face. "Don't you *realize* what's involved in selecting a wedding dress?"

Alex rolled her eyes. "Yes," she maintained. "I try on another bunch of dresses, find one that I like and pay the bill for it. And voilà, I have a wedding dress."

"Ha!" The single syllable put-down echoed. "Selecting a dress is just the beginning. Then there're the fittings and finding appropriate bridesmaid dresses that are decent but don't overshadow the dress you've chosen, plus—"

Alex sighed, obviously struggling to maintain her good humor. "Wear whatever you like that's pretty," Alex told her sister breezily.

"It's not that simple," Stevi insisted, her voice rising again to a shriek. "We have to be coordinated. Alex, you not having a dress yet is a serious, serious problem. Why aren't you taking it seriously?" Stevi wanted to know, unable to fathom how her sister couldn't understand the situation and its repercussions.

Cris could see that Alex's smile was forced, as well as fading around the edges.

"Maybe because I'd like to look back on

this time fondly and not remember it as the beginning of my terminal ulcer."

Exasperated, Stevi turned toward Cris. "Help me out here," she begged.

Cris shook her head, letting Stevi know that her younger sister wouldn't get what she was hoping for from her. "I'm on Alex's side."

Almost at the end of her rope, Stevi threw up her hands. "Look who I'm asking for help—Elopement Girl." She leveled a long, hard look at Alex, hoping to bully her into complying. "Okay, this is how it's going to play out. You are taking the rest of the day off and we are going from bridal shop to bridal shop until you find the right dress."

Alex shot her down with two words. "Can't, Stevi." She paused for half a second to nibble on a strawberry that had been a leftover after Cris finished making a shortcake. "I've got to meet with the local fire inspector for his monthly walk-through of the premises. He's coming this afternoon." Glancing at Cris, she said, "This is good," referring to the strawberry.

Cris nodded in response, smiling, while Stevi ordered, "Reschedule."

Again Alex turned her down. "Can't. He's fitting me in as it is. The inspector's really busy."

Stevi held up the pad she'd drafted into service to keep tally of all the things that had to be attended to in order to pull off a proper wedding reception. "And you're not?" she demanded, stunned.

Alex's smile stretched to the limit as she patted Stevi's cheek. "That's what I have you for, so you can handle the details."

"Details?" Stevi cried incredulously, obviously offended.

"You'll beat them down into the tiniest pieces. I have faith in you, Stevi," Alex told her.

Just then, the door leading into the kitchen swung open and Alex's fiancé walked in. Dressed in the casual clothes he favored, Wyatt also sported a wide, amused grin. He was leading in a heavyset, jovial-looking woman. The woman appeared intent on absorbing her surroundings, much like a Hoover vacuum cleaner.

"I can hear you two all the way in the main room." Wyatt paused to give Alex a quick one-armed hug and brush a kiss to her lips. "Oh, you're here, too," he realized, noticing Cris for the first time. "You I didn't hear," he confessed with a laugh.

No mystery there, Cris thought. "That's because your future wife and Stevi don't really leave much room to get a word in edgewise."

Wyatt's grin grew wider. "Tell me something I don't know."

"How about something *I* don't know," Alex prompted, exceedingly comfortable where she was—in the middle of Wyatt's semiembrace. Who would have thought that would ever be the case, she couldn't help musing, given the antagonism that had dogged their every encounter for so many years. "Like who your friend is," she clarified.

Alex looked pointedly at the woman Wyatt had brought. Whoever she was, she seemed unusually at ease amid a crowd of strangers. A long-lost relative? She knew Wyatt didn't have any immediate ones, what with both his parents gone and his being an only child.

Wyatt laughed, realizing his oversight. "Oh, sorry," he said, apologizing not just to Alex but to the woman he'd brought with him, as well. "I guess I was just so over-whelmed with seeing you after our lengthy five days' separation I forgot my manners."

The corners of Alex's mouth curved tol-erantly. "Sarcasm was never your long suit, Wyatt."

"Maybe not," he allowed, "but wit always was. We promised no ego crushing for the first six months, remember?" he reminded Alex, feigning seriousness as he gazed at his almost bride with affection. "Anyway, this is Myra McGregor—my wedding present to you," he ended with a flourish.

"I hate to be the one to have to tell you," Cris interjected, "but human trafficking is frowned on around here these days."

Wyatt laughed. "Your sense of humor's coming along, Cris," he told her with ap-proval, nodding and looking pleased. "Let me try again," he said to Alex. "Myra's a costume designer, the proud recipient of three Oscar nominations as well as one lovely little golden statuette for last year's three-hour epic *The Empress Catherine*."

"Congratulations," Alex told the woman, instinctively knowing that congratulations were in order. "I'm sorry if I didn't recognize your name right off the bat. I don't get time to go to the movies very often," she confessed. However, she knew that Wyatt, an acclaimed, accomplished screenwriter, moved in those kinds of circles, and people whose likenesses flickered on the screen were among his friends.

The woman smiled at her. "That's okay. It's not like I'm a household name—yet," she qualified pointedly, obviously intending to be just that someday.

A woman after her own heart, Alex thought. But that still didn't explain why Wyatt had brought her to the inn with him.

Alex looked at her fiancé. "I'm sorry if I'm being a little obtuse, but why are you giving me Myra?"

"Myra's going to design your wedding dress. She's amazingly fast and her team of seamstresses will take whatever sketch you approve and make it a reality quicker than you could thumb through an oversize issue of *Brides Beautiful Today,*" he told her.

Stevi closed her eyes and breathed a sigh of relief. She exhaled so loudly it sounded like the fall wind picking up and preparing for an assault. Opening her eyes again, she focused them on her future brother-in-law and declared with complete sincerity, "Thank God for you, Wyatt."

He laughed, getting a kick out of the entire event. He'd never seen Stevi so emotional and at the same time so pushy.

"Glad to help. You forget. I grew up with the four of you." He glanced at Alex. "I know how uncompromising my future wife can be."

"Not uncompromising. Just right," Alex corrected. "And 'right' doesn't compromise," she informed Wyatt, smiling but firm.

He looked at Cris. "Have that inscribed on my tombstone when the time comes, please."

Cris merely smiled, humoring him the way she was humoring everyone else in the room right now. She wanted to do whatever it took to have them moving on their way so she could reclaim her space. She had another meal to prepare for.

"I took the liberty of making a few sketches on the drive down from Los Angeles," the designer told Alex.

"You drove here? Why didn't you fly?"

Alex asked. Wyatt always flew between the two cities.

"I don't fly," Myra said. "And Wyatt was nice enough to humor me."

"*Nice* had nothing to do with it," Wyatt denied. "I wanted to be sure I got her here for you."

"And on that note," Myra said, jumping right in, "if you have a few minutes, I'd like you to look over the sketches so I know if I'm on the right track."

Alex appeared a little uncertain. "I'm waiting on the fire marshal," she began, and although she'd be on the premises, she didn't want to be distracted while making her all-important selection.

"Cris or Stevi can give you a holler when he gets here," Wyatt said, slipping his hand down to the small of her back and lightly moving her in the costume designer's direction. "Besides, this shouldn't take too long."

"Can't I just look at the sketches here?" Even as Alex asked, they heard a child of one of guests squeal, effectively making Myra's point for her.

"It's better if you review them without any distractions," Myra assured her.

"We're asking for ten minutes, Alex," Wyatt pointed out, "not an eternity."

"We?" Alex echoed, surprised. She turned to him. "You intend to come along?"

"Well yeah, sure." Wyatt didn't see what the problem was. "After all, I'm the one who talked Myra into coming here."

Without saying a word, Alex eyed her sisters, who then joined ranks to act as a human barrier between Wyatt and her, as well as the costume designer he'd driven all the way down here.

"No, you're not helping her," Cris informed him politely but firmly.

"Why not?" He appeared puzzled at the sudden opposition from the sister he considered the most levelheaded and logical. He and Cris *always* agreed on things. What was going on here?

As if reading his mind, Stevi answered his question. "Don't you know it's bad luck to see the wedding dress before the wedding?"

"But she's only got sketches," he protested, waving a hand at the stack Myra was holding.

"Doesn't matter," Stevi said, digging in. "Presumably, one of the sketches will be of the dress Alex'll be wearing when she marries you."

Why would seeing a sketch of her dress change anything? He'd already been through the worst of it and still wanted to marry Alex.

Wyatt made an appeal to everyone's common sense. "I know every one of Alex's bad habits—"

"What bad habits?" Alex deadpanned.

He ignored the bait and pressed on. "And I still want to marry her, so what could happen if I see a silly little sketch?" he wanted to know.

"Lot's wife had the same attitude when she turned around for a last-minute look to see what was happening to her city, Gomorrah," Stevi told him, stubbornly standing her ground.

Raising his hands in a blatant show of surrender, Wyatt took a symbolic step away from Alex and the woman he'd talked into creating a one-of-a-kind wedding dress for her.

"I forgot how formidable you can all be when you join forces. Is Ricky around?" he asked, looking about the immediate area. "I need another male to bond with."

"Ricky's at the playground," Cris said, adding, "Andy didn't have any classes today and she took him to the playground right after his kindergarten class let out. But my dad's out back," she volunteered cheerfully.

"And Shane's over at the new wing, working," Alex said. She deliberately ignored the censoring look that Cris shot her, but the partial exchange wasn't lost on Wyatt or the others.

"Shane," Wyatt repeated. "He's the guy you used to go to school with, right?" he asked Cris.

Cris shifted ever so slightly, getting back to cleanup and avoiding Wyatt's eyes. "No, I went to high school with his sister, Nancy. Shane was a couple of years older than us."

Wyatt nodded, absorbing her explanation. "I knew there was some connection," he said. "I just didn't get it quite right."

Raising her head, Cris pointedly eyed her elder sister. "Shouldn't you let Myra get started showing you the sketches or making new ones if you don't see anything you like? Not to take Stevi's tone—"

"What's wrong with my tone?" Stevi demanded

Cris went on as if nothing had been said to interrupt her. "But you *are* cutting it a little close."

"Finally!" Stevi cried, vindicated. And then she added her voice to Cris's. "You are, you know. And if you're not careful, you'll wind up walking down the aisle naked."

Wyatt began to laugh. "Now that's something I'd pay to see."

"Save your money," Alex said crisply. "It's not going to happen. I'll pick out a dress today."

Wyatt tried vainly to appear disappointed and wound up laughing even harder as he accused her of being a spoilsport.

"Let's go, Myra," Alex said to the short, full-figured woman beside her as Stevi buffered her other side. "Before I come to my senses and change my mind about marrying this man."

"Start drawing fast, Myra," Wyatt called after the departing women.

Cris laughed and shook her head. "You sure you understand what you're getting into?" she asked him with the affection a sister might have for an older brother.

That was how she had grown to regard Wyatt because of all the summers he and his father had spent at the inn. The two had come year after year, after Wyatt's parents split up because of a career that kept his father away from home for roughly half the year, if not more.

Wyatt nodded in answer to her question as he grinned broadly. "Looking forward to it," he confided. "But please don't tell Alex. It'll give her too much of an upper hand and I'd like to start out even, if at all possible."

Cris couldn't help thinking that Alex was one lucky woman, and she envied her just a little. Envied her the joy and comfort that lay ahead of her.

But she still couldn't resist teasing. "You know where to find us when you need a shoulder to cry on," she told him.

"Yes, I know." Wyatt nodded, playing along. "I've got a fairly decent sense of direction."

"That was a really nice thing for you to do," she said, referring to the designer he'd brought out to tackle Alex's wedding dress. "You're a good guy, Wyatt."

"I did it mostly to keep peace in the family," he told her frankly. "This way, Stevi doesn't drive Alex crazy, dragging her from bridal shop to bridal shop and Alex doesn't strangle Stevi, trying to get a little peace and quiet."

"Still," Cris said, inclining her head, "it was nice of you."

"Myra said dealing with a real person instead of a Hollywood personality would be a pleasant change. See, everyone's getting something out of it," he told her. "Even you." When she looked at him quizzically, he explained. "If Alex picks out a dress, Stevi's happy. If she's happy, she won't be in here complaining. See how it works?" he asked.

"Yes, I do." Cris took the mop out of the closet, wet it and began to wipe down the floor. "And just between the two of us," she confided, making short work of the floor beside the stainless-steel worktable, "I'll be glad when this wedding is finally over and things are back to normal." *Please, God,* she added silently, the specter of what her former in-laws wanted to talk to her about never far from her thoughts.

"Whatever that is," Wyatt interjected. He'd always maintained that one man's normal was another man's insanity.

"Touché," Cris acknowledged with a smile.

Rather than walk out of the kitchen and leave Cris alone, Wyatt decided to stay put a few extra minutes.

Cris assumed he'd stuck around for the only reason men converged on kitchens to begin with. "Are you hungry? Is there anything I can get for you?" she asked.

"I can wait until Alex and Myra are free," he said, choosing to eat with them rather than by himself. He debated for a moment, thinking that Cris might just prefer he didn't go digging in anything. But he truly cared about her the way he did about Stevi and Andy, and since he was marrying into the family, it gave him a right to butt in.

So he did.

Coming closer to Cris so he didn't have to raise his voice, he said, "So, tell me about this Shane guy."

Cris almost dropped the pot she had taken

from the shelf beneath the worktable. Only quick reflexes saved it from clattering to the floor.

"What?"

He went on to explain his reasoning. "Well, Alex seems to think something's there," Wyatt noted. "Otherwise, she wouldn't have brought up his name."

"You mean something between Alex and Shane?" Cris asked, trying to get Wyatt's question squared away.

Her question, so foreign to his straight line of thinking, threw him. "What?" And then he realized why she had made her mistake. "Oh. No. No way," he said, uttering more feeling with each word. "I mean between you and Shane. I saw how Alex glanced in your direction when she said his name. For what it's worth—and I'd stake a lot on Alex's people instincts—*she* thinks something's happening between you. Now, what do *you* think? Is there?" he asked, looking pointedly at Cris.

Cris shrugged, doing her best to appear completely in the dark about any implied meaning.

"Not in the way you might mean and certainly not in the way Alex would like. Since you and she got together and decided to get married," Cris explained, "Alex thinks everyone should pair off and get married. Shane and I share a history—a very small history," she emphasized so no mistake was made this time. "Nancy McCallister was one of my best friends in high school and I was over at her house a lot. Sometimes Shane was there. But I was his little sister's friend and a guy that age wants nothing to do with 'children,' which was what he considered Nancy and me."

She deliberately left out the part about dating him a couple of times, afraid she'd lose her last ally if she mentioned that. Especially since it hadn't really meant anything at the time, she silently insisted. After all, both she and Shane had gone on to marry other people, right?

"Alex and our dad hired Shane to do some work at the inn and he's doing it. We've exchanged a few words during this time. End of story." She dusted off her hands to make a point.

The expression on Wyatt's face as he regarded her said, *Is it?* But he said nothing other than, "Well, let me go find your dad before I decide to pop in on Alex and take a look at Myra's sketches. See you later."

She nodded, already busy.

Not to mention relieved there would be no more questions from anyone.

At least until "later."

CHAPTER NINE

"Need any help in here?"

Preoccupied and in her own little world, struggling very hard not to let her thoughts run away with her, Cris had to exercise strict control not to jump at the sound of the deep voice behind her.

Taking a steadying breath and congratulating herself for not letting out a squeal, she turned from her worktable.

She was surprised on two counts to hear Shane asking her a question. First, because he was at the inn so early on Thanksgiving Day—it was barely eight o'clock in the morning—and second because he was volunteering to help.

"Why aren't you home, sleeping in?" she asked.

Because of the holiday the noise associated with renovations would definitely not be welcome today, so she assumed Shane would be still snug in his bed, sound asleep. Mike used to love to grab a few extra winks whenever he could.

"Never got into the habit," Shane answered simply. "Between having to get up early as a kid if I wanted to see the inside of our one bathroom ahead of my parents, my brother, Wade, and especially my sister, Nancy, and then being in the army, which didn't exactly worry about any of us getting our beauty sleep, waking up at dawn sort of became second nature."

He peered around the kitchen. The work surfaces were either devoted to pans filled with various items that needed baking or bags of foodstuffs that had yet to be prepared, like the twenty-pound bag of Idaho potatoes. What the kitchen didn't have, other than the two of them, was people.

"So," he continued, now looking at her, "you didn't answer me. Need any help?"

She deemed it a strange offer, coming from him, considering what Shane had told her the other day. "I thought you said you really didn't know how to cook."

"I don't," he replied honestly. "But I've got a strong back and I can fetch and carry any heavy object you might need taken from there to here—like those potatoes," he said, nodding at the huge bag on the counter. "I also know how to peel and chop—as long as you don't want anything to look perfect," he remembered to qualify. "Because I don't do perfect."

She liked the way he didn't dress things up. "That's okay, neither do I."

His eyes washed over her slowly enough to warm her from the roots of her hair to the tips of her toes. She had to remind herself to breathe.

"I find that hard to believe," he told her, his voice lower than a moment ago.

"If you want to do something for me, I could stand to have that window opened," she said after a beat. "With all this moving around and boiling—" she nodded toward the stove top, which, at the moment, was embarrassingly off "—it's gotten a little warm in here."

The way she asked, if there hadn't been a window in the kitchen, he would have created one for her on the spot. But, luckily, there was.

"One open window coming up," he told her with a sharp nod.

Shane made his way over to the room's one window, which was located between two rows of cabinets and directly over the industrial sink.

After flipping the lock that held the two panes together, he slid one pane over the other, then opened the window as wide as possible without physically popping the pane out.

"Too much?" he asked, glancing over his shoulder at Cris.

She crossed to the window and stood beside him. The cool air felt good on her face.

"Probably in a few minutes," she conceded. "But right now, it's wonderful." She paused to take in another long breath, to fortify herself as well as calm some unusually jumpy nerves.

Cris closed her eyes for a second. She could feel a cool breeze ruffling the bangs that were drooping over her eyebrows and were partially in her eyes. She knew that her cheeks were a deeper pink than they normally were and here in the kitchen at least she could attribute the change in her complexion to the heat rather than to the true cause.

When she opened her eyes again, Shane was looking at her. "Something wrong?" she asked.

Since he'd come into the kitchen, no one else had walked in. "Are you handling all this alone?" he wanted to know.

Considering the large meal she'd be making, that she was manning the kitchen by herself did seem incredible.

"Where's your part-time help?" Shane asked her.

"Well, I told Jorge to take some time off so he could go to Taos, New Mexico, and spend Thanksgiving with his family. And both Eddie and Sylvia," she said, mentioning the other two people who worked at the inn's kitchen occasionally, "had family coming to visit them, so I gave them both the four-day weekend off, too."

Her generosity to others left her without much generosity for herself. "Leaving you with all the work," he concluded.

"Don't make it sound like I'm Cinderella," she said with a pleasant, amused laugh. "I managed to get a jump-start on pretty much everything last night. All the desserts were done then, and the more complex side dishes. I'm just about finishing up with the sausage and salami stuffing, then that'll be ready for the oven. As for the turkeys, they're all prepped and ready to start roasting."

That was when he noticed the shallow baking pans—four in all—on the back workbench, lined up side by side like incredibly pale, potbellied soldiers waiting to be called up and pressed into service.

"Wow, those turkeys look big."

"That's because they *are* big. All four are around twenty-five pounds each," she told him.

"A hundred pounds of turkey," he marveled. That could go a long way to feed an awful lot of people in his estimation. "Just how many people are you expecting?"

Cris smiled at the question. She realized that there was a lot of food here, especially given the number of people who'd be sitting in the dining area in another ten hours.

"I like being prepared—just in case something goes wrong with one of the turkeys," she confessed.

He supposed she had a point—but in all

likelihood, nothing would go wrong. Which brought him to the next problem.

"What if you have a ton of leftovers?" he asked. "There are only so many ways to fix turkey leftovers before the very thought of them makes you want to run screaming into the street."

Preparing the honey glaze she was going to use for the baby carrots, Cris stopped and grinned at him. "I can't picture you doing that. And nobody's going to be running or screaming—because if we do have any significant amount of leftovers, you're free to take them to the homeless shelter where you volunteer. I'm sure that the shelter could always use some extra turkey."

Shane stared at her, surprised that she actually remembered he volunteered at the shelter. With most people, the information went in one ear and out the other. "That's really very nice of you. I appreciate that—and so will the people who run the shelter."

Cris shrugged off the compliment. "I'm just being practical," she corrected. "I don't like the idea of wasting food by throwing it out." And then a question occurred to her. "How come you're not there today?"

Instead of answering her, he had a question of his own, asked only partially in amusement. "Is that your way of telling me you'd rather not see me hanging around here?"

"No, I like having you here." The second the words were out of her mouth, she realized what they had to sound like to him. And she didn't want Shane thinking she was trying to crowd him. "I mean, to help with all this. I'm just surprised they didn't ask you to come in to the shelter today."

That was a simple enough question to answer, he thought. "Because on the big holidays like Thanksgiving and Christmas and Easter, the homeless shelter has more than enough volunteers helping out. Celebrities like to show up on those holidays, show how charitable they really are—*especially* if they just 'happen' to have a photographer in tow, ready to snap photographs of them doling out food, playing with little homeless kids, things like that. Makes them feel better about themselves and gets them good publicity at the same time."

She was amazed that he didn't sound cynical about this. It was almost as if he was saying it didn't matter *why* the celebrities were there. As long as they were helping out, any reason that brought them there was okay.

"I need that bag of potatoes moved from the counter to the table," she told him, pointing to where she wanted the twenty-pound bag deposited.

"Told you my strong back would come in handy," he said.

"Why do you do it?" she asked him suddenly, curious about his reasons.

Shane raised one eyebrow, puzzled at the question. "Didn't you just tell me to put the bag—?"

"No, I mean why do you volunteer at the shelter? You don't have a photographer snapping your picture," she said. She went back to making the carrot glaze.

He shrugged, as if past examining the reasons. "I do it because there aren't enough people at the shelter to help out the rest of the time." Having hefted the bag over to the table, he dusted off his hands one against the other. "It takes a lot to run a place like that and the funds are unbelievably limited," he said. "And I do it because when I look into some of those faces, I think, 'there but for the grace of God go I.'"

She stopped working and looked at him. "When were you ever in a situation like that?"

"If you mean about to forfeit the roof over my head because I lost my job, never," he told her flatly. "If you're talking a hopelessness eating away at my gut and driving me into a bottomless pit of despair, then the answer is not as long ago as you might think."

She could almost feel the pain he must have experienced, pain as keen as a sharpened carving knife. "You mean when your wife was killed?" she asked, her voice dropping to a whisper, as if she didn't want to offend Shane by asking too many questions or speaking too loudly.

"Yeah," he answered crisply. "I mean then." He struggled with the old feelings, trying to keep them behind the protective glass where he'd finally managed to place them. It didn't protect his feelings, but *him*.

Shane thought of just dropping the subject and picking a happier topic. But his wife deserved better than being swept under a rug and forgotten.

That was why he finally said in a voice that was distant but filled with pain nonetheless, "She was pregnant at the time."

Cris's mouth dropped open as disbelief echoed through her. "My God," she murmured. "I didn't know."

He nodded, his eyes unfocused for a moment as he looked back into the past. "She was. The doctor who tried to save her—to save them," he corrected himself, "said it was a boy. I would have had a son if... He would have been around Ricky's age."

Cris stopped dicing the celery stalks she had nervously started dicing when he'd begun talking about his wife, put down the long knife and crossed to him.

Placing her hands on his shoulders, she wished she could take away some of the pain, pain that in a way they shared because of the abrupt manner in which they had both lost their spouses—suddenly and all too soon. A death swiftly delivered that gave no time to prepare for the loss and left you faced with endless time to endure the pain.

Such pain was hard to crawl out from under, harder still to move beyond to make a new life. She'd done it because she'd had family to support her and she knew she couldn't rob her son of the only parent he had left by wallowing in self-pity.

But that was her. Who had Shane had to help him through this valley of endless pain?

"I am so very, very sorry, Shane," she told him, wishing the words could somehow better convey the extent of her empathy.

Shane saw her eyes misting over, and witnessing that hit him in a very sensitive, unprotected spot. He could *feel* tears gathering, threatening to blind him. If he wasn't careful, any second now his sorrow would demand release.

"Cris," he whispered, placing his hands on her shoulders. His intent was to move her and the unbound sympathy she offered away, at least keep it at arm's length so it wouldn't breech his suddenly fragile wall of defense and cause him to shed the tears he had kept back all these long, lonely years.

Instead, for reasons he did not understand, he drew her closer to him. Moved his hands from her shoulders to her hair, threaded his fingers through the silky blond lengths and brought his lips down to hers.

IT HAPPENED SO fast it took Cris's breath away. Yet at the same time she felt it was transpiring in slow motion, with every movement forever, indelibly, imprinted on her brain.

She felt her pulse beating quicker, echoing a pounding heartbeat.

He'd caught her completely by surprise, but rather than draw back, she melted into the kiss, absorbing it, above all enjoying it to a surprisingly pleasurable degree.

Not only that, but she found herself an active participant in it. She wove her arms around Shane's neck, drawing him closer, pulling herself to him as well as she stood on the very tips of her toes to do so.

She could honestly say that she didn't know what hit her—but she knew that she wanted it to continue. Wanted to offer him comfort, wanted to—at the same time—draw comfort from him.

For however long or not long it was going to last—and she had lost the ability to gauge time—she wanted to remain in this strange, protected place where nothing bad could come anywhere close to her.

HE HAD BEGUN it and it was up to him to end it—even if he didn't want to. Then he would be forced to apologize for something he didn't want to apologize for.

Because it was something he had done almost reflexively—certainly without any forethought. He hadn't known he was going to kiss her until *after* he was kissing her.

But, dear Lord, it was the best move on autopilot he had ever made, he thought even as he tried—without success—to break contact with Cris. Tried to release her, even though holding her was the sweetest, most soothing thing he had done in so long he couldn't even remember the last time he'd felt close in this way. In all honesty he couldn't remember the last time he had felt anything remotely like this.

Because he could swear there were rays of sunshine piercing the corners of the darkness that his soul had sunk into.

Finally, with supreme effort, Shane drew back, his breathing far from regular even though he tried to control it.

He struggled to frame an apology. Nothing came to him, least of all remorse. Still, that didn't change anything.

"I guess I should say I'm sorry."

Cris caught her lower lip between her

teeth the way she used to when she was an undecided teenager. Her bright blue eyes rose to his.

"Are you?" she queried, mentally crossing her fingers because, in spite of his statement, she knew what she wanted to hear.

He was aware he was supposed to say yes, he was sorry. Very sorry. But he wasn't sorry, "very" or otherwise. And he had no desire to lie to her. That would have been easier; it just didn't seem right. So he answered, "No."

He wasn't prepared to see the smile that bloomed on her lips. Was even less prepared to hear her say, "Me, neither." And was caught completely off guard at the burst of happiness he felt in his heart at her answer.

CHAPTER TEN

ANDY DELIBERATELY CLEARED her throat before she spoke.

"Sorry, am I interrupting something?" the youngest of the Roman sisters asked.

She looked from Cris to Shane, a somewhat surprised yet pleased look slipping over her fine features as she took in the scene and put her own spin on it.

Five years Cris's junior, Andy was in her last year at the University of California San Diego, the same university Alex had attended. In Alex's case, she'd gone to this San Diego campus rather than any of the other UC locations because she wanted to remain close to home. Their father had fallen seriously ill at the time and she had taken it upon herself to run the inn until he could get back on his feet.

Andy, on the other hand, had opted for UC San Diego because it was convenient for her. She crashed with friends who lived on or near campus when she was so inclined. The rest of the time she came home, because home, despite her restless soul and everything she might gripe about, was all-important to her. Her independence and the support she felt derived from this one source.

She might enjoy talking about soaring high, but she would be the first to acknowledge how welcome she found it to know a safety net was strung out wide beneath her—just in case she lost her footing in life and fell.

To her great amusement, she saw her sister and the hunky general contractor who'd been working on the inn's latest addition spring about two feet apart, as if she'd wedged a hot poker between them.

She supposed, given the circumstances, an apology was in order.

"I'm sorry. I was just coming to see if you needed a hand or two. Looks like you don't," she observed, unable to hide her delight. It was about time Cris came out of that self-imposed shell she'd been occupying for so long.

"Your sister had something in her eye. I was just trying to help her get it out," Shane told Andy without missing a beat.

He felt that offering an explanation was the least he could do. After all, if he hadn't initiated the kiss, he and Cris wouldn't have been caught in a compromising position

"All better?" Andy asked, looking pointedly at her sister despite the seemingly caring question.

Andy wasn't buying Shane's narrative for a second, Cris thought. Her eyes shifted to Shane. The excuse he'd tendered had risen effortlessly to his lips. Was he just good under pressure—or was his dissembling a sign she should take serious note of?

Did this tall, handsome, thoughtful man utter lies without a second thought, or was it just this once, to cover for her and, to his way of thinking, protect her reputation? Not that they were doing anything so terrible. After all, they were two consenting adults and the only thing they'd consented to was a harmless kiss.

Or was it? a little voice in her head whispered, playing her personal devil's advocate. *Was it all that harmless? Then why are your*

insides all scrambled as though they'd just taken a couple of spins in an industrial food processor?

Sometimes, Cris couldn't help musing, she was her own worst enemy. She ordered herself to stop overthinking everything before she wound up with an ulcer.

"Yes," she answered her sister brightly. "Shane got whatever had fallen into my eye out, so I'm 'all better' now." She deliberately blinked her right eye several times for Andy's benefit. "It feels just fine again."

"Small wonder," Andy murmured just loud enough for Cris to hear.

Andy was *really* tempted to comment that she'd never seen the approach Shane was using to remove pesky dust from an eye. Clearly mouth-to-mouth resuscitation had more unique uses than enabling the victim to breathe again.

But maybe that was pushing the envelope a bit too far and she liked Shane too much to embarrass him or put him on the defensive. So, though it was never easy for her to hold her peace, Andy dropped the subject—for now.

"Oh" was all she said in response.

"You mentioned something just now about volunteering," Cris prompted, trying her best to divert the conversation to a topic she could better control.

Andy snapped to attention, remembering her initial purpose in seeking Cris out.

"Yeah, I thought that since you were being so magnanimous and giving everyone who normally helps out in the kitchen the long weekend off—and since I was home and temporarily fancy-free—" she lifted her arms above her head like a pirouetting ballerina "—I'd see if you needed someone to pitch in. But—"

"No buts," Cris said, cutting in before Andy could rescind her offer. "The more the merrier. As long as Dad or Alex doesn't need you out front, you're more than welcome to get all hot and sweaty here in the kitchen."

Andy's eyes all but danced as she listened to her sister. "Oh, so it's the kitchen that's getting you so hot and sweaty?" she asked with a very mischievous smile on her face.

"Yes, Andy," Cris said deliberately, enunciating each syllable as she fought not to glare at her sister or give her a dressing-down. Doing that in front of Shane would make them both uncomfortable. "It's the kitchen. The temperature here has to be at least fifteen degrees higher than in the rest of the inn."

Andy glanced at the area above the sink and did a bad demonstration of keeping her tongue in her cheek. "With the window open, too. Guess we have our very own example of global warming, huh?"

Cris fixed her sister with a penetrating look. "Are you here to help or harp?"

"Good one, Cris." Andy could appreciate skillful wordplay, even if it was being used against her. "I'm here to help. Use me any way you want," she offered glibly, putting her hands out, wrist-side up.

With Andy's hands held that way, Cris wasn't sure if Andy wanted to be put to work, or handcuffed as punishment for being so glib.

"Please don't tempt me like that," Cris warned her sister. "I'm only so strong."

Andy inclined her head, a grin curving her lips. "Duly noted. Okay, where do you need me?" she asked, looking around the kitchen as if an assignment would just pop up.

There was still so much to choose from, it was difficult deciding, Cris thought. The kind of help Andy could offer came under the heading "grunt labor," same as Shane's. Andy's culinary skills left a lot to be desired.

Most likely Shane, who was looking on in amusement, was a better cook than Andy—even if he was as bad as he said.

"I need a bunch of the carrots peeled," Cris finally said.

"And those are—?" Andy asked, leaving the end of her question dangling as she looked around the immediate area again and saw nothing

"Right over here," Shane told her. He led Andy over to the unopened sack of baby carrots by the supply closet. "I noticed them when I got the potatoes," he told Cris in response to her impressed expression.

"So she's already enlisted you into her kitchen corps?" Andy asked as she stood back, allowing Shane to heft the bag in question up for her. He placed it on a secondary worktable.

"I volunteered," he corrected, "just the way that you did."

Andy glanced over her shoulder at her sister, her light blue eyes dancing with what appeared to be enjoyment.

"And here I was, feeling sorry for you. That'll teach me." She laughed.

Cris didn't want to be the object of pity: she wanted Andy helping simply because she wanted to.

"Thought you might want to help just because it's a family celebration. The kind of thing you can look back on and talk about when you're surrounded with grandkids of your own."

Andy laughed as she shook her head. The scenario was way too perfect. "I don't know what kind of grandkids you have in your world, Cris, but in mine, kids tune out everything and everyone except for their peers and whatever they want to hear. By the time they're ready to listen to stories from their parents or grandparents about 'the olden days' the person who can tell them those stories has passed on to the next world."

"She always this cheerful?" Shane asked

Cris good-naturedly as he nodded at her sister.

"Just this semester," Cris answered. "It's the psychology course she's taking. I think it's called Cynic 101."

Andy frowned as she raised her eyes to her sister's face. "I can hear you, you know."

"That's debatable," Cris answered. Andy only heard what she wanted to hear. "By the way, what have you done with your nephew? I thought you got the short straw and were going to watch him while I prepared the customary fantastic Thanksgiving dinner," she said, doing her best to sound serious.

"Dad volunteered to take over with Ricky. I think he misses hanging out with the little guy since Ricky started kindergarten. Apparently Ricky's teacher wants them to make a diorama depicting the first Thanksgiving feast and bring it in right after the holiday."

"Why would she want it *after* Thanksgiving?" It seemed odd to do it after the fact. To her it seemed only natural to move on with the course work.

"Maybe she wants to extend the season," Shane suggested.

"Maybe. So is Dad helping Ricky with this diorama?" she asked Andy.

Andy shook her head. It was part of the reason she'd pulled a disappearing act. "Stevi started to take over, doing this elaborate scene with feathers and all—you know how Stevi can get."

"Tell me about it." Cris laughed.

"Well, Dad said that Ricky needed to do it himself—like any teacher would believe a five-year-old could put together that scene Stevi created," she said, rolling her eyes. "Anyway, I just quietly got out of there before things could get really ugly."

Cris suddenly came up with an idea. "Why don't you go back and take Ricky to Ms. Carlyle's room?" she suggested.

The moment Cris's words were out, Andy's expression lit up like a skylight at high noon. "Of course," she cried. "Why didn't I think of that?"

"You can't be brilliant all the time," Cris deadpanned.

Andy pursed her lips in a semipout. "Now who's being sarcastic?"

Cris feigned innocence. "I haven't got the foggiest. Now go knock on Ms. Carlyle's door and find out if it's all right to bring Ricky over to her. Personally," she confided, "I think she'll love it. Nothing like feeling useful, no matter what your age."

"On my way," Andy declared, already crossing to the kitchen door. "Oh, and don't feel bad if you don't leave me anything to do here," she interjected, waving a hand about the kitchen.

"No chance of that," Cris called after her. "Still lots to do for when you get back."

"Ms. Carlyle?" Shane asked the moment Andy had hurried out of the kitchen. "Who's that?"

A fond smile curved Cris's lips as she got back to peeling potatoes.

"Ms. Anne Josephine Carlyle," Cris said, "is the inn's only permanent guest. She taught elementary school—fifth grade mostly from what she said. Every summer she and a bunch of her teacher friends would get together and tour some European country or other, then come to the inn to spend a week before returning to their respective schools in the fall.

"Little by little, the group of friends grew smaller and smaller. As Ms. Carlyle became less mobile, her stays here became longer and longer. When she finally retired and most of her friends had either died or moved away, she spent more and more time here. Eventually, she asked Dad if she could live here permanently."

Cris smiled as she recalled the story that had been told and retold so often she knew the words by heart. "Ms. Carlyle made it sound like she was the one doing him a favor, keeping one of the rooms leased all year round. She told him she would only agree if he gave her a 'reasonable' rate, reasonable in this case being cheaper than the surrounding inns.

"As if Dad would ever take advantage of anyone." Cris slipped another fully peeled potato into the giant bowl of water to keep the potato from turning brown. "She's been here a number of years now and to be honest, when I was growing up at the inn, Ms. Carlyle was the first guest I ever took any note of. She's actually a walking treasure trove of the inn's history if you ever want to know anything. When Wyatt was writing that book about the inn Uncle Dan had started, he relied a lot on Ms. Carlyle and her incredible memory."

"Remind me to pick up a copy of that book," Shane told her.

Maybe she was reading something into his words, but it seemed to her Shane was really interested in a subject dear to her heart. That made it all rather nice, she thought.

"I'll lend you my copy," Cris offered. "By the way, it was very sweet of you coming to my 'rescue' like that."

Shane looked at her quizzically for a second before he realized what she was talking about. "Oh, you mean saying that you had something in your eye." It wasn't so much a question as checking that he'd recalled the right scenario.

Cris nodded. "You're pretty quick on your feet," she commented. "Get much call for being so creative?" she couldn't help asking. The question had been nagging at her since he'd come up with the excuse.

"If you're asking whether I make things up a lot, no, I don't. But your sister had a very amused expression on her face and I couldn't tell if you wanted her to know that

I'd kissed you. I figured that this way, telling her or not telling her would be up to you.

"But as a rule, no, I don't fabricate things. Or lie," he spelled out in case that was still in question.

"Lies only get you into trouble because half the time you can't remember what it was you lied about."

She paused for a moment, weighing the issue—and drew a conclusion. "I take it you're not speaking from experience."

He laughed shortly. "Not directly, no. But Wade, my brother, he tended to be very, um, 'creative.' It got him into a lot of hot water more than once. He liked me to cover for him and used to get really bent out of shape when I didn't. Eventually, though, he came around to my way of thinking."

"Your sterling example rubbed off on him?" Cris asked.

"No, I think it was more a case that he couldn't keep his stories straight and one of the women he was stringing along decided to give away all his possessions. He was engaged to her at the time and she found out he was also 'engaged' to three other local women. Anyway, she gave his things to Good Will, including his car. He got the car back, but not the girl. That was when he decided that just maybe he needed to clean up his act."

"And did he?" Cris asked, fascinated despite herself. She'd long since stopped peeling.

"As far as I know. Besides, if he ever has a relapse, his wife will probably kill him. Eva loves him a lot, but she's not one of those little meek ladies who'll suffer in silence. If Eva's suffering, *everyone's* suffering," he told her with a warm laugh.

"Sounds like you get along with her," she noted.

He grinned, recalling a few incidents. He'd been best man at his brother's wedding. "I do."

How hard it was when family members moved to different states. She knew how lonely she'd be if her sisters moved away. "Too bad you can't go back east for the holidays."

His eyes when they met hers held a meaningful look. "There are compensations," he assured her.

The remark warmed her heart for more than the next few hours.

CHAPTER ELEVEN

CRIS LOOKED AROUND at the people seated on both sides of the long, festive table.

A sense of pride, combined with a wave of sensitivity and sentiment that she usually didn't allow herself to feel, whispered through her.

She savored the feeling for only a brief moment. It was all the time she would allow herself.

Normally she kept a tight lid on sentiment since it usually made her feel weepy.

There was nothing to cry about today. She had her family around her, which she knew made her luckier than a great many other people. In addition, her beautiful son was bright and healthy and he was surrounded with people who absolutely adored him.

Right now, life felt perfect. And that was what scared her.

As a child, she'd noticed that whenever

things felt perfect, suddenly something would happen that would shoot arrows of pain through her.

The very first time was when her mother had unexpectedly been taken from her. The next was when her father fell ill and she'd been so afraid that they would lose him, as well. Terrified, she'd kept vigil over him until, mercifully, he'd gotten well again.

After that, everything had gone along smoothly for a long while. Better than smoothly. She'd married Mike and their joy when she found out she was pregnant had been off the charts.

When he was killed a few weeks later— her letter to him about her pregnancy in his pocket for good luck, of all things—she didn't think she would ever recover, ever ascend from the abyss she was free-falling through.

But slowly, inch by inch, locking away all her emotions until such time as she could deal with them, Cris had struggled to make her way back up to the land of the living. Back to being a productive person, a loving daughter and sister. Above all, a loving, caring mother. She did it for Ricky and for

Mike, who would have been disappointed in her if she'd given up.

Having her heart savagely carved up taught her two things: never take happiness for granted and always be aware that life can change in less than a heartbeat, which meant that the solid ground beneath her feet could become a sinkhole faster than she could even envision.

And that had her thoughts turning toward the pending visit from her in-laws. What could they possibly want to talk about regarding Ricky's future?

Before fear could rise up and cut off her air supply, she pushed the thought away, sticking it into an imaginary, airtight metal box. She'd deal with it when the time came. Nothing she could do about it now—except pray every night that she was overreacting.

With effort, she focused on her immediate surroundings.

This afternoon, the dining area was full. Her entire family was gathered at the main table, along with Wyatt, who would soon become the brother she never had, and Shane.

Shane's presence gladdened her but made her feel uneasy at the same time. She liked him—*more* than liked him if she was truly honest with herself—and because she did, she was waiting for some nebulous, awful *thing* to happen that would wound her almost mortally.

Just like all the other times.

Her sisters had set the tables and pitched in to bring the food out for both the family and the inn's guests.

Today, everyone was family.

That was the message Richard Roman wanted to convey and his daughters made certain that it came across.

When Cris was finally done in the kitchen, Ricky and Shane had each taken one of her hands and pulled her into the dining room despite her protests that she felt she'd left something undone.

"Whatever it is, it'll keep," Shane had assured her.

Ricky had tugged at her apron strings, undoing them, and Shane had deftly tossed the apron aside the second it had loosened.

"Time to start," her father had called out just as she was escorted into the dining area.

Shane and Ricky buffered her on either side as they made her take a seat. Cris perched on the edge of the chair rather than sitting back, a sure sign that she intended to spring into action as soon as she was able or the need arose.

"You heard the man, Cinderella," Shane told her. "Officially time to start Thanksgiving."

"That's not her name," Ricky told Shane, laughing at Shane's "mistake." "Her name's Mama. I forget her other name, but she likes me to call her Mama. She's not your Mama," he confided to Shane in what could be best described as a stage whisper. "But you can call her that if you want 'cause she'll answer. But she won't answer if you call her Cinderella," the boy informed his friend seriously.

Shane grinned as he inclined his head in a little bow. "I stand corrected."

Ricky frowned. His expression said he thought adults were strange, even the really nice ones.

"No, you don't," Ricky argued, mystified. "You're sitting."

"Ricky, it's not nice to correct grown-ups," Andy warned her nephew in as stern a voice as she could manage while stifling her laughter.

"Shane doesn't mind, do you, Shane?" the little boy asked, seeking backup and confident he would get it.

And he did.

"Nope," Shane answered genially. "How else am I going to learn?" he wanted to know, clearly amused.

Just too good to be true, Cris thought, looking on and taking in the exchange between her son and Shane. She struggled to brace herself for the inevitable letdown, but she was at a loss as to which direction it would come from.

"Hey, I think the gravy's missing," Stevi said, looking around the table as she did a quick mental inventory of what should be on the table and what was still waiting in the kitchen to be pressed into service.

At the mention of the gravy, Cris sprang from her seat. "I'll get it," she said to everyone at the table and no one in particular.

She would have made a beeline for the kitchen if strong fingers hadn't suddenly tethered her wrist. She found herself looking down into Shane's chiseled face. He was smiling at her, but with a steely smile that said he'd made up his mind and no amount of her talking would change it.

"No, you won't," Shane told her evenly. "You're going to stay right here, even if I have to tie you to your chair. *I'll* go for the gravy."

"Easy, big fella," Stevi teased, rising to her feet as if she intended to push him down by herself if he didn't obey. "You don't know where anything is in the kitchen. I'll get the gravy."

"No, neither one of you will," Alex told them both.

Still standing, Stevi propped one fisted hand on her hip in the universal body language sign of impatience. "Why? Because you don't think I can find anything?" she wanted to know.

"No, because the gravy bowl is right there, behind the baked yam and apple dish," Alex pointed out. "But just for the record, Stevi, you *do* have trouble locating things."

"Girls." Richard's soft, even voice commanded their attention. "This is a day for giving thanks, not for giving your father a headache with your squabbling."

"Yes, Dad." Alex pretended to meekly

withdraw from the confrontation, as did her sister.

"And I for one," Richard said, gazing at the people seated at his table, "am extremely thankful for each and every one of you. I feel very blessed right now. It's been a good year and it promises to be even better," he said, looking directly at his late best friend's son, "with Wyatt officially joining our family."

"He was always part of the family," Stevi was quick to remind her father.

"Even when I was verbally sparring with Alex?" Wyatt teased. To him, they had *always* been his family. Richard and his daughters were his anchor, even when he'd been too young to realize it.

"*Especially* when you were verbally sparring with Alex," Cris assured him. "We were all secretly cheering you on."

"Thanks," Alex said wryly, pretending to be miffed.

"As a matter of fact, at times, I think we all liked you better than we liked Alex." Stevi slanted a whimsical glance at Alex and deadpanned, "No offense, Alex."

"None taken," Alex answered, mimicking her sister's tone.

"I think you should just say grace, Dad, and start carving the turkey while there're still no visibly wounded at the table," Andy prompted. "They can't talk if their mouths are full of food."

"Very good idea," Richard declared with a laugh. Turning toward his grandson, who was seated beside his mother, he said, "Ricky, would you like to say grace for us?"

Ricky grinned, raised his small chin and declared, "Grace."

"Very funny," his mother said tolerantly. "And now say it seriously."

"Yes, ma'am." Her son folded his hands before him, bowed his silken head as he closed his eyes—and remained silent.

"Out loud," Cris prompted. "Say it out loud."

Ricky turned his head slightly as he opened one eye and looked at her, puzzled. "God can hear me."

"Very true," Shane agreed, making eye contact with the boy. "But we can't. Why don't you share it with the rest of us?" he suggested.

Ricky's face lit up instantly. "Sure," he cried, eager to please the new man in his life. Taking a breath, he bowed his head again and this time, in a clear, strong voice, said, "Thank you, God, for taking care of us, for Aunt Alex and Wyatt getting married and thank you for my new friend Shane. Oh, and for him making Mama laugh again. I like hearing her laugh. Amen," he announced, then looked up. "Can we eat now?" he wanted to know, stressing the last word.

"Yes," Richard answered his grandson as he rose to his feet, taking the freshly sharpened carving knife in one hand. He steadied the turkey with the matching fork in his other. "Everything looks perfect, Cris," he told her. "As usual."

"I had help," Cris replied, deflecting the compliment so that it encompassed her sisters as well as Shane. "Everyone pitched in."

Richard nodded. It might have been her imagination, but she could have sworn her father was eyeing Shane as he told her, "Things always go faster when you have help."

"I don't know about that," Alex said. "I think Cris breathed a huge sigh of relief when I bowed out this year to cover the desk."

"I did not," Cris protested. "At least, it wasn't a 'huge' sigh," she corrected.

"We'll leave the comment right there," Wyatt interjected. "I know how these things can escalate, given half a chance."

"Good idea," Richard agreed. "All right," he declared, glancing around at his family, "who wants dark meat?"

"YOU ALREADY DID enough helping me prepare the meal—you don't have to clear the table," Cris told Shane two hours later. He was following right behind her with a tray full of dishes, his destination the dishwasher.

"I know," he replied cheerfully, "but I want to."

"Nobody wants to face dirty dishes if they can help it," Stevi told Shane, coming up next to him as she brought in another load of plates from the dining area.

All the guests had eaten, expressed their thorough enjoyment of the meal and cleared out, leaving the leftovers and the empty plates for Cris and whoever volunteered to help her with them.

Although she was pleased when Shane began to pitch in, Cris felt obligated to tell him he could sit this out because he was, after all, more of a guest than not and guests were supposed to relax after the meal, pick a favored corner of the main room and quietly doze off in one of the wing chairs.

"Okay, I don't exactly like KP," Shane confessed, "but I do want to show my appreciation for the meal and especially for being allowed to share in the company." He paused for a moment as he rolled up his sleeves. "I want you to know that this was one of the best Thanksgivings I've ever had. Certainly the best one I've had in recent memory."

Cris laughed softly and shook her head. "Well, I'll say this about you—you certainly have a low threshold when it comes to appreciation."

Shane looked at her as he picked up the top plate from the tray he'd brought in and passed it to her. His fingers brushed hers. Both she and he felt the light current that passed between them.

"Not so low," he contradicted. "Actually, I consider it relatively high."

"Well, that's my cue to leave," Stevi announced, beginning to back away.

Cris gazed sharply in her sister's direction. She wasn't fooled for a second. "Ha! Anything is your cue to leave."

Stevi stopped in the doorway, sparing her a single glance over her shoulder. "I can take back the dishes I just brought in," she threatened.

"Just go play with my son," Cris told her, waving Stevi off to the main room. As Stevi disappeared, Cris turned to Shane. "You're free to leave, too, if you like. I was serious earlier. You've more than done your time."

He made no attempt to leave. Instead, he picked up another plate and passed it to her. "You have a hard time accepting help, don't you?"

There was no point in arguing with him over that one. "We're all control freaks in my family to greater or lesser degrees," she admitted. "As for accepting help, it's just more of a case of my not expecting it."

"That should make it all the more pleasant for you to be on the receiving end when it does happen," Shane noted. "I speak from experience."

"Oh?"

"Yes. I didn't expect to even have turkey for Thanksgiving, much less the kind of feast you put together."

Despite warning herself not to get drawn in, Cris knew her curiosity had been aroused. She had to ask, "What were you going to have?"

He shrugged. "I didn't think that far ahead. But since you inquired, I probably would have stopped at one of those little sandwiches-to-go shops and gotten whatever was at the top of menu." As his words echoed in his head, Shane stopped and laughed at himself. "I guess now is when you'd hear sad violin music if this were a made-for-TV movie."

For a moment, he had pulled her in. *Really* pulled her in. When she let her defenses down, she could feel everything the person she was empathizing with felt.

"Well, I don't know about violin music," she said, trying to shake off her empathy for him, "but it sounds pretty sad to me. I'm glad you decided to spend the day with us."

"As I recall," he reminded her, "it wasn't

actually my decision—it was more of a command performance."

"Regrets?" she asked, unable to gauge by his tone if he had them or not.

A smile curved his mouth. "Only if you don't let me show you my gratitude by letting me help you with cleanup."

Cris laughed—and then recalled what Ricky had said during grace. Shane did make her laugh, she realized. "Well, when you put it that way, I guess I really can't just send you away, can I?"

He shook his head. "Nope. And I wouldn't go even if you did."

She looked at him for a long moment. There was something in his voice, something that held a promise—but of what, she couldn't pinpoint. "Are we still talking about the dishes?"

"Sure," he replied, a bit more breezily than she would have thought him capable of. Was he pulling her leg or hinting that not everything was visible on the surface? "Why?" he asked her in all innocence. "What else would we be talking about?"

The smile on his lips now was a teasing one, as if he was just barely holding back a laugh, and a secret he wasn't about to share—yet.

Just your imagination, Cris. You're tired and you've been working too hard. There's no hidden meaning behind his words, no multiple choices to weed through.

What you see is what you get.

If only...

"Not a thing," she replied. "Why don't you start rinsing the plates and getting them ready for the dishwasher while I consolidate the leftovers?"

"I'm yours to command," he answered glibly, taking his position by the sink.

Cris stopped herself before her imagination could take off again. But, she quickly discovered to her growing dismay, reining in her thoughts after hearing such a leading line wasn't at all easy.

CHAPTER TWELVE

"Please, Mama, pleazzze?" Ricky begged.

The little boy had been singing the same refrain, in varying intonations, off and on since the morning after Thanksgiving. That had been five days ago.

The plaintive supplications all revolved around getting Cris to go looking—and ultimately, of course, buying—a Christmas tree for the inn.

"Christmas is almost *here,*" Ricky pleaded, stressing the last word as he followed her around the kitchen the way he seemed to have been doing every day of late.

Even when one of his aunts or his grandfather managed to distract him with something for a short while, he always made his way back to her and picked up where he'd left off as if no time had gone by in between.

Ordinarily, Cris dearly loved Ricky's company, even when she was busy preparing meals for the guests. She could multitask with the best of them.

But this morning she'd picked up her cell phone to discover a message that she'd been trying not to think about even as she was dreading it. Her former mother-in-law had called her to say they would be arriving sometime during the week.

When she'd attempted to return the call, she'd gotten the woman's voice mail and heard a robotic voice informing her that the phone was off. There was no point in leaving a message—Marion MacDonald never returned messages—so Cris didn't.

More fluttering butterflies in her stomach turning into oversize objects.

Why now? Cris couldn't help wondering. The last time she'd seen the couple, Mike's mother had made no effort to hide her anger at Cris for refusing what Marion had informed her was a "very generous offer." The offer entailed Ricky and Cris moving into their home—a place that could only be referred to as a mansion.

They had assumed it was a done deal and were really taken aback when Cris had turned them down, saying her life was here at the inn. She'd gone on to tell the couple they were welcome to visit Ricky any time they wanted to.

That was almost a year ago, and except for the Christmas and birthday cards, both with sizable checks made out to the boy, she hadn't heard a word.

Once again, even as she was enjoying the peace and quiet, she should have known it was too good to last.

Well, she'd find out what was going on soon enough, she told herself. She saw no reason to ruin Ricky's joy in the approaching holidays just because of her own anxieties.

In a patient voice, Cris pointed out, "Christmas is more than thirty days away."

Ricky climbed onto one of the stools that was pushed up right beside a worktable, so that his face was closer to hers. "But we gotta find the tree, bring it home and decorate it. That takes a whole bunch of time," the little boy insisted. "All the big good ones will be gone if we don't hurry up and buy one."

"Then we'll get a medium-sized good one," she told him, slicing potatoes for her own recipe of potatoes au gratin. She might as well have suggested drowning Santa Claus in the ocean from the look of horror that descended over Ricky's small face.

"No!" Ricky cried, appalled. He jumped off the stool as Cris left the worktable to get more potatoes. "It's gotta be a big one. Grandpa said it does."

"Grandpa only said that because he knows that's what you want," Cris tactfully pointed out. "If you wanted a big blue monster standing in the middle of the main room instead of a Christmas tree, Grandpa would go along with that, too."

Ricky grinned broadly. "I like Grandpa."

"I bet you do." Cris couldn't help but laugh. "Because you've got him tied around your little finger."

Ricky looked down at his hands, examining them in mystification. "No, I don't, Mama. Grandpa's too big for my fingers."

Cris laughed again. She'd forgotten how literally words were taken at that age. "Sorry, little man, what was I thinking?"

"I dunno," Ricky answered honestly, as if his mother had asked a legitimate question. "So can we go? Puh-leezze?"

"Honey, I have to finish making lunches first," she said.

Jorge had watched this scene in silence, amused by the boy's unwavering persistence, but now he had to speak up.

"I can take over, Miss Cris," he volunteered. Back from his visit with his family, he was relaxed and more than ready to return to work. "You go tree hunting with the boy here," he told her, fondly ruffling the boy's hair.

Ricky's eyes almost sparkled. Cris looked at her assistant uneasily. She didn't want him getting in over his head just so she could indulge her son.

"Are you sure, Jorge?" she asked, studying his face. I don't like just running off and leaving you like that."

Jorge shrugged dismissively. "You're only going for a couple of hours, right? There aren't that many Christmas tree lots in the area, are there?"

It was a rhetorical question. Each year, there seemed to be fewer and fewer lots with a significant number of trees. She thought about it for a moment.

"No, I guess not," she agreed.

"See?" Ricky cried. The point he'd been trying to hammer home had been made for him. He flashed a smile of thanks to Jorge. "If we don't go now, there won't be any big trees left. Grandpa and Shane said we *needed* a big tree in the main room," he insisted.

"Somehow, I don't remember Grandpa and Shane wording it that way," she told the boy.

But she could remain immune to his big blue, supplicating eyes for only so long before she finally caved. Plus, Cris wasn't sure if her nerves could withstand another day's verbal assault. Not in her present state of barely controlled agitation. She decided she needed something to distract her.

"Okay, we'll go pick out a tree," she said to Ricky, surrendering.

Rather than remain at her side, Ricky immediately dashed for the swinging kitchen door.

"Hold it, little man," she called after her son. "Wait for me. You're still not old enough to drive by yourself."

"I know *that,* Mama," he told her, irritated she'd made that sort of mistake. "I'm going to get Shane. He said to tell him when you were ready. He's coming, too," he added, in case his mother had forgotten.

She'd thought that Shane's initial offer to accompany them on their Christmas tree quest had just been one of those throwaway offers uttered on the spur of the moment—in this case to placate Ricky—and then immediately forgotten.

"Honey, Shane's busy," she gently reminded her son.

"Not too busy for me," Ricky replied. "He said so, Mama. Just now."

About to give Shane an alibi, Cris stopped cold and stared at her son. "Just now?" she echoed.

"Uh-huh," Ricky testified solemnly, his head bobbing emphatically. "He's waiting for me to tell him what you said. I'll tell him you said yes!" With that, Ricky pushed open the swinging door with both hands and raced out.

Watching, amused, Jorge deadpanned, "Kids, they grow up so fast these days."

"A little too fast if you ask me," Cris murmured. If she didn't know any better—and she wasn't entirely sure that she didn't—she would have said her son was manipulating her. That, as well as bringing in reinforcements.

"You're certain you can handle this?" she asked, giving Jorge one last chance to change his mind.

"Go, before I become insulted," he told her.

"Gone," she declared.

BY THE TIME Cris had taken off her apron, dragged a hand through her hair to make it a bit more presentable and gotten her purse from the tiny back office off the kitchen, Ricky was waiting for her in the main room—and he had brought his "reinforcements" with him.

She felt bad. Shane probably thought that because Ricky was the boss's grandson, he had to indulge the little boy.

"Look, I know you have a lot to do, Shane," she began, giving him the option of bowing out, "so don't let my son guilt you into coming with us."

"No guilt involved," Shane assured her pleasantly. "Unless it's the kind that comes from playing a little hooky."

Ever curious, Ricky queried the word he didn't understand. "What's hooky?"

Cris patted his shoulder. "Nothing you should know about."

Shane realized he probably shouldn't have said that. "Sorry," he apologized.

Cris waved off the apology. "Don't worry about it. Having kids around is a constant learning experience for everyone," she told him. "Nobody expects you to know everything. But really, I meant what I said. If you're busy, you don't have to come."

"To be honest, I was looking forward to it," he said, echoing his earlier words. "It's been a while since the holidays actually meant anything to me besides having a cold beer and watching *It's a Wonderful Life* in the original black and white."

The admission caught her by surprise. And pleased her. It cast him in an even better light. "You like *It's a Wonderful Life?*"

He was aware that liking the movie wasn't exactly macho. "Not something I should admit, huh?"

Cris immediately shook her head. "No, no, I think it's wonderful—"

"No pun intended?" he asked with a grin.

"Absolutely none," she said, and laughed. "That just happens to be one of my all-time favorite movies. Alex always rolls her eyes and sighs every time she catches me watching it," she confessed. "But I can't help it—and Dad enjoys it. I thought he was the only male who did," she admitted.

"I like it, too!" Ricky declared, eager to join the exclusive club.

"Only male over the age of six who did," Cris corrected. "Speaking of my father, let me see if he can come with us."

"Um." Shane held up his hand, stopping her in her tracks. "I already checked with him. He said we should go without him."

"You checked with him?" she asked, puzzled. Why would he do that?

"Well, I didn't want to take off without making sure it was all right with him. I didn't want your father thinking I'd gone AWOL. That's 'away without leave,'" he explained to Ricky.

"Oh," the little boy said wisely, nodding as if Shane's explanation had just said cleared up everything for him.

Cris couldn't help smiling. Not at the look on her son's face because he pretended to understand what AWOL meant, but because Shane had been thoughtful enough to explain the word, speaking to him like an equal rather than an adult talking down to a child.

That Shane treated Ricky with thoughtfulness and respect meant the world to her.

She forced herself back to the topic at hand. "Is my father sure?" she asked Shane.

"That's what he said," he answered, then offered, "but we can postpone going if you'd rather he come with us."

She shook her head. "I don't think Ricky can hold out another five minutes," she said, putting her arm around the boy's slender shoulders affectionately, "much less another day, and heaven knows that *I* can't take another day of Ricky following me around, pleading to go Christmas tree shopping." She looked down at her son. "No offense," she said.

The small face puckered in consternation, as if a new puzzle challenged him. "What's that mean?"

"It's something people say when they don't want to hurt someone's feelings with something they just said," she explained.

"You could never hurt *my* feelings, Mama," he told her.

"I could," she contradicted. "But just by accident," she added quickly in case her admission could undermine the boy's confidence and feeling of well-being.

"Well, then, unless there's someone else you'd like to bring along," Shane told her, "I think we're ready to go."

"Yeah!" Ricky all but cheered.

Trying vainly not to laugh, Cris linked her fingers with her son's. "I'd say all systems are go, Captain, wouldn't you?"

Shane smiled and his smile felt like sunshine to her. Once again a part of her felt disloyal to Mike for reacting to Shane this way. But once again she knew Mike would want her to be happy, to move on. Except, she just couldn't do it. Not with a clear conscience, no matter how much the rest of her might yearn for contact with the opposite sex.

With Shane.

"Absolutely," Shane was saying to her.

Absolutely, she echoed in her mind.

THE FIRST LOT Shane drove them to in his navy blue oversize truck had a number of nice specimens, but although they were all bushy in appearance, most of the trees were eight feet or less.

"Nope, too short," Ricky pronounced over and over again each time his mother or Shane presented him with a candidate.

Finally, after they had spent close to an hour wandering among the rows of trees, a crestfallen Ricky looked up at the man he had all but adopted and said, "Our Christmas tree isn't here. Let's go somewhere else."

"Sounds like a plan," Shane answered, then looked at Cris to see if she was on board with this plan or whether he had to talk her into it.

"You heard the man," she said, then added to underscore her son's cavalier instruction, "we need to find a second Christmas tree lot."

THE SECOND LOT stood where a pumpkin patch once had. This lot had fewer trees to offer than the first lot, and although some of the new candidates were upward of eight feet, they were on the sparse side.

"We could always glue in extra branches,"

Cris suggested. When her son looked stunned at the prospect, she quickly assured him, "I'm just kidding, honey. If it's okay with Shane, we can try to find a third lot."

"Hey, fine with me," Shane said with a magnanimous shrug.

"Just as long as you remember," she told Ricky, trying her best to sound at least semi-stern with him, "it's three strikes and we're out."

"No tree?" Ricky asked, horrified at the mere suggestion.

"Yes, tree, but we go back to the first lot and get a really plump shorter one," she quickly explained to prevent his face from falling to the ground. "What the tree will lack in height, it'll make up for in width."

Ricky was having none of it. "We'll find our tree," he told her confidently.

"Yeah, 'Mom,'" Shane chimed in, playing along. "We'll find our tree."

She laughed, shaking her head as Ricky once again climbed into the car seat she'd transferred from her vehicle to the back of Shane's truck.

"Nice to be traveling with such men of confidence," she said to Shane.

He liked her laugh, he thought for the umpteenth time. Liked the way the corners of her eyes crinkled when she smiled like that.

Liked, he thought as he got in behind the steering wheel of his truck, sharing space with her *and* her son. For the first time in a long time, he felt part of a family—even if it was just for an afternoon.

"I saw a lot being set up this morning when I drove down to the inn," he told them once he turned his key in the ignition. "It looked like they might have a pretty good selection. Want to try there?"

They certainly had nothing to lose. "Lead the way," Cris told him.

THE LOT SHANE took them to had three times as many trees as the first lot they had hit. The trees were arranged in no particular order, so finding what Ricky called "the right tree" would take some time.

Ricky vetoed a number of trees that both his mother and his new best friend showed him.

"He's pretty picky," Cris apologized after yet another rejection had taken place.

As always, Shane pointed out the silver lining in less-than-favorable circumstances.

"Hey, he knows what he likes and that's a good thing. He won't grow up to be one of those vacillating people with no opinions, no backbone."

"He won't survive to adulthood if he keeps running ahead of me like that," she threatened, realizing that Ricky had managed to race ahead once more. This time, he'd disappeared from view.

"Ricky, you know you're not supposed to run off like that!" she yelled, picking up her pace to try to catch up to the boy. "Ricky!" she cried again when he didn't reappear or call out an answer. "Where are you?"

The next second, to her surprise, Shane ran past her, then turned the same green corner Ricky just had. The aisle was a treasure of tall, bushy trees.

"Ricky," he called sternly. "Listen to your mother."

"Here!" Ricky called back. "Over here! Come quick!"

CHAPTER THIRTEEN

"ISN'T IT BEAUTIFUL?" Ricky asked excitedly, glowing with pride as if he had not only been the one to discover the tree but had also had a hand in its creation.

"It is that," Cris had to admit.

To show her son she wasn't just humoring him, she circled the tree slowly and realized, astonishingly, that Ricky had found a tree completely without the usual "bald" side. It was the closest thing to a perfect Christmas tree that she had seen in a long time.

"And tall!" Ricky crowed, looking from his mother to Shane. "Isn't it tall, Mama?"

"Absolutely," Cris answered.

The majestic tree appeared to be at least ten feet in height, if not taller. As she examined it, though, she worried that the tree's very height might present a problem.

Concerned, she looked at Shane. "Isn't this a little too big to get into your truck?"

Shane did his own reconnoiter of the tree.

"Offhand, I'd say you're right, but where there's a will, there's a way," he told her, thoughtfully regarding Ricky's tree.

"'Will' only goes so far," Cris pointed out pragmatically.

Shane's eyes met hers. "Depends on whose will it is," he replied.

Something told her that mild mannered though Shane seemed, he could undoubtedly be extremely stubborn if the occasion called for it.

"Maybe you're right," she conceded.

Ricky glanced from his mother to Shane and back again, clearly having gotten lost in their exchange.

But the way the small boy saw it, only one thing was really important. "We're getting this tree, right, Mama? Right?" he repeated, his eyes begging her to agree.

"It does look pretty perfect," Shane told her, adding his vote to Ricky's.

No way she was going to rain on her son's parade—especially if she had no backup.

"It does," she concurred, at which point Ricky, obviously feeling that the battle for the tree had been won, began whooping.

However, Cris wasn't finished. "But we'll have to either hire a truck to get this tree back to the inn, or have the guy running the lot deliver it for us."

Shane grinned at her. She could tell by his expression that he didn't agree with her. The first words out of his mouth told her she was right. "You're underestimating Yankee ingenuity—and the strength of my truck. We can take this home ourselves."

"Yay!" Ricky cried, punching the air with a doubled-up fist the way he'd seen athletes do after scoring a wining point.

"Why don't we hold off on the cheering until after we've done it?" Cris cautioned.

"All right, let's go find the guy who runs the lot," Shane said gamely—but it was Ricky who started to run off to look for the man.

Shane managed to grab the boy by the hem of his jacket to keep him from taking off.

"Hold on there, guy. Unless you've got a credit card your mama didn't tell me about, I'd say you have to wait for her to come with you before this can be a done deal."

Deflated, Ricky sighed. "Okay. C'mon,

Mama," he urged impatiently. "Before someone else buys our tree!"

Cris had a feeling that it was probably useless to point out to her son that the lot was still empty and most people usually bought their trees closer to Christmas. Logic was not about to curb her son's eagerness or his impatience.

So she took his hand in hers, saying, "Well, we can't have that, can we?" and together with Shane they went in search of the man operating the lot.

"Hey, mister, we found our tree!" Ricky announced to the lot manager, whose ID tag on his chest proclaimed his name to be Howard.

"You did?" Howard asked with a toothy grin. "Good for you. Which one is it?"

"The big one!" Ricky declared.

"We'll show you," Cris interjected, knowing that given her son's height, Ricky's description applied to practically any of the trees.

"Lead the way," Howard stated, gesturing in the general direction they'd come from.

With Ricky straining against the hold his

mother had on his hand, the boy led them to the Christmas tree he'd fallen in love with.

"That's a beauty, all right," Howard proclaimed expansively.

Cris had a feeling that had they pointed to a scrawny twiglet, Howard would have said the same thing with the same amount of enthusiasm. However, the man *was* likable, so she didn't feel he was just trying to snow them.

Rather than speaking to either adult, Howard looked down at Ricky. "This the one you want to take home with you?"

Solely by Ricky's expression, he had his answer long before the boy cried, "Yes!"

Howard then turned to Shane and asked, "You folks sure you've got enough room for this in your house? These trees look a little smaller outdoors than they really are."

"Actually, it's for the main room at an inn," Shane explained.

The information aroused Howard's interest. "Oh? Which one?" he wanted to know.

"Ladera-by-the-Sea," Cris said, studying his expression, wondering if he was genuinely interested or was just saying whatever came to mind to appear even friendlier than he already did.

Howard smiled, nodding. "I'm familiar with it," he told them. "I drive past it on my way to work. Nice place," he added amicably. "So do you two own it or just run it?"

"My grandpa owns it," Ricky spoke up, appearing very proud of the fact.

"Pretty bright boy you have there," Howard commented, turning to Shane.

"Thanks, but I can't take any credit for him," Shane answered. "He's her son. I'm just the hired muscle who's driving back the tree."

Cris looked at Shane, her expression saying he was a little more than that.

"Oh." Howard laughed, his ruddy complexion turning just a little ruddier at his error. "Sorry, didn't mean no harm by what I just said. Natural enough a mistake to make," he told them. "You three act like a family, so I just thought—"

Blushing, Cris cut in, "Do you think there would be any trouble taking this tree on the back of his truck?" she asked.

"Tell you what, let's go have us a look-see," Howard offered, glad for the shift in topics.

Shane led the lot manager over to where he had parked his truck.

They were still some distance away when Howard began to nod. "Looks fine to me," he said. "Shouldn't be a problem getting that tree up on your truck. One word of advice, though. If I were you, I'd drive real slow. Otherwise, either the tree—or your truck—is gonna wind up being airborne."

"Why?" Ricky asked, his eyes huge at the prospect of a flying truck.

"Air gets between the truck and your tree," Howard answered. "Even at regular speed it's gonna start lifting you up. Going slow is your only option."

Ricky turned toward Shane, excitement written all over his face. "Can we do that? Can we see if your truck flies?"

"Not this time," Shane said. "We want to get the tree to the inn, not to Oz. Right?"

"Right," Ricky agreed with a quick nod. Only Cris caught her son's slightly wistful expression before it vanished.

"So should I write this up?" Howard

asked, dutifully turning toward Cris for an answer.

Cris nodded. "Please," she urged. Ricky fairly jumped up and down as they went back to Howard's register to finalize the transaction.

Once the tree was purchased, Shane and the lot manager began the somewhat awkward task of preparing the tree for transport. The task went a great deal faster than Cris had anticipated, despite Ricky's help.

The tree, which measured closer to eleven feet than ten, was expertly bound and carefully tied to the truck, its trunk secured to the top of the truck's cab and the rest of the tree attached to the vehicle's body.

The process, from start to finish, took close to an hour. But by the end of it, the tree gave every indication that only a capricious twister could separate the tree from its mode of transport.

"Now remember, you drive real slow, like you're trying to maneuver that truck of yours on eggshells without breaking them," Howard told them, leaning in and addressing his words to Shane, "and you should do just fine."

"Eggshells," Shane repeated, banking his amusement. He nodded. "Got it."

Howard stepped away from the truck. Once the man was clear of his vehicle, Shane started it up and made his way out of the lot at what felt like an inch at a time.

"Good thing this lot isn't all that far from the inn," Shane commented, seriously thinking that he could walk at a faster pace than he was driving. "Otherwise, we'd get there in the middle of next Tuesday," he cracked. And then he smiled to himself.

"What's so funny?" Cris asked, curious.

"I've never driven this slowly before, not even when I was learning how to drive." He shook his head as he struggled to hold back laughter. "If I was going any slower, I'd be going backwards."

"Can we go backwards?" Ricky piped up, tickled by the idea.

Rather than tell the boy no, Shane said, "Maybe next time."

The answer seemed to placate Ricky.

That it did was not lost on Cris. "You've really got a way with kids," she told Shane.

Shane took the compliment in stride, saying, "I should."

"Why's that?" she asked. Was Shane good with kids because he had one of his own whom he hadn't mentioned? Was there a child out there with his face? Had he deliberately not told her about being a father? But why would he keep that secret from her?

His simple answer caught her off guard. "Because I was one myself."

"Most everyone was," she pointed out. "And few of us act accordingly."

That was because most adults practiced amnesia, he thought, forgetting all about the path that had brought them to their present station in life.

"Yeah, well, I remember what it was like. Distinctly. And I use that," he added. "Most people can't remember what they had for breakfast, much less what it felt like to be a kid and have their opinion dismissed out of hand because they're young." Since he was driving slowly enough to be outpaced by a snail with a limp, he spared Cris a look as he continued. "I've got a great sense of empathy. It lets me put myself in most everyone else's shoes."

"Doesn't that pinch?" Ricky wanted to know.

"Nope," he replied to the boy as if his question had received serious consideration. Ricky ate up the respect.

"Even women?" she queried, wondering just how far Shane was willing to carry this. The man was definitely beginning to sound too good to be true—and she knew that when things were too good to be true—they usually weren't.

"My rule applies to people, not gender," he answered. "Far as I know, women are people just like men."

"*Not* just like men," she emphasized. "But we definitely are people," she said and laughed, agreeing with his basic theory.

Silence accompanied them for a couple of minutes. Now would be the best time to clear the air, Shane decided. Turning toward Cris, he said, "I hope you didn't get too upset."

She hadn't gotten upset at all, nor was there any reason to, as far as she could see. "Over what?" she finally had to ask.

The topic made him feel antsy. "Over that lot manager, Howard, thinking we were a married couple."

Cris shook her head in response to his statement, then said, "It didn't bother me."

Actually, it did. But not because she was offended by the mistake. What bothered her was how much being mistaken for a married couple had actually *pleased* her.

She wasn't supposed to feel that way about someone else when Mike couldn't feel anything at all anymore, she silently lectured herself. Alex's lecture about regaining complete control over her life notwithstanding, Cris felt bad that she was attracted—*strongly* attracted—to another man.

She had no time for that, no place in her life for that, she insisted. Raising Ricky and working at her father's inn was all she had time for, nothing more.

Certainly not a man, no matter how nice he seemed or how much her son liked him.

So why was she trying to justify her feelings to herself?

"Good, I wouldn't want you to be offended," Shane was saying.

"That never even crossed my mind," she said, then decided that they needed a change in topic before Shane could discern the truth—that she liked that they looked like a family to other people.

Liked it so much that for a few seconds back there, her imagination had created lovely scenarios that truly warmed her heart and made her smile.

Cris deliberately looked at her watch. "How much longer do you think it'll take us to get back to the inn?"

"Why? Getting impatient with the slow pace?" he couldn't resist asking. He had to admit that it felt as though they weren't even moving at all.

"It's not that."

And it wasn't. There was precious little she enjoyed more than being in the cab of Shane's truck with him behind the wheel and her son sitting in back.

But right now something else was bothering her. "I should be getting ready to serve dinner to the inn's guests," she told Shane.

"Why don't you call and tell your father we're on our way, albeit slowly, and ask him to have Jorge get started without you?"

"Right."

How come she hadn't she thought of that,

she chided herself. It was as obvious as the nose on her face.

Because, Cris was forced to admit, being in this situation with Shane and Ricky seemed to have done away with a large portion of her brain. In Shane's company, she'd ceased being the practical, logical creature she'd been brought up to be and became a woman who suddenly relished living in the moment. *Enjoying* the moment and trusting the rest of the day to take care of itself.

Get a grip! Cris ordered herself.

She pulled out her cell phone, pressed the numbers on the keypad and called her father at the inn.

Alex answered the landline, the only number she had for her father at the inn. Old-fashioned almost to a fault, her father didn't own a cell phone. He considered it a frivolous indulgence, although he thought nothing of calling her and her sisters on their cells.

That was her next goal, she decided. Get her father a cell phone and teach him how to use it.

"Ladera-by-the-Sea," Alex's melodious voice stated. "How may I help you?"

"Alex, it's Cris," Cris began. "Tell Dad that we found a tree—"

"*I* found the tree, Aunt Alex!" Ricky called out loudly so his aunt could hear.

"It's almost eleven feet tall," Cris continued. "And we're on our way home with it, but because it's so big and we have to drive slowly, it might take us a while to get there. Could you have someone ask Jorge to stay and start dinner for the guests? I'll get there as soon as humanly possible," she added.

"Jorge—dinner—right. Shouldn't be a problem," Alex said, "if I can catch him before he leaves. He just punched out a couple of minutes ago. Anything wrong on your end?" she asked as an afterthought.

"No, but if we drive fast, the wind might catch the tree and we just might end up flying off with the tree."

"Not a pretty image, although I'm sure Ricky would love it," Alex said with a laugh. "Let me see if I can catch Jorge before he pulls out of the parking lot."

The next minute Alex was gone, the hum of a dial tone replacing her voice.

As she closed her cell phone, Cris mentally crossed her fingers. If Alex didn't catch

Jorge before he left, she herself would be facing a lot of hungry, less-than-happy guests of the inn.

As if reading her mind, Shane assured her, "Don't worry, we'll be there sooner than you think."

She smiled at him, once again grateful for his words of encouragement.

CHAPTER FOURTEEN

"Stop fidgeting, Ricky," Cris said as she tried to undo the seat belts tethering him to his car seat. "I can't get these straps to open if you keep wriggling like that."

"Hurry, Mama, hurry," Ricky urged, his feet swinging impatiently as he watched the front door of the inn. "I wanna tell Grandpa we got the Christmas tree!"

"I have a feeling he probably already knows," Cris responded, working another strap free.

"But what he doesn't know is how perfect the tree you picked out is," Shane told the boy, bringing Ricky's wide grin back with that small compliment.

"He's really gonna be surprised, huh?" Ricky asked eagerly, his eyes dancing with excitement and anticipation.

"You bet he is," Shane agreed with the same measure of enthusiasm.

Shane really had the inside track on being on the same wavelength as her son, Cris thought. She felt bad that Shane had never had the chance to be a father to his unborn child. He would have been fantastic—and his baby would have been one lucky little boy.

"There, you're free," Cris announced, lifting the boy out of the seat and placing him on the ground.

Ricky's feet hardly seemed to touch the concrete before he took off, running up the front steps.

"Grandpa, Grandpa, come quick! Come see our beau-ti-ful Christmas tree," he called as he yanked open the front door and charged into the inn.

"Be careful not to run into anyone," Cris called after her son, then turned to look at Shane. "Boy, if I could just tap into that energy for a day," Cris said wistfully.

"You're not exactly a slouch in the energy department from where I stand," Shane told her.

"Smoke and mirrors," she confided with a self-deprecating laugh. "Beneath is a very, very exhausted woman."

"Well, you could have fooled me," Shane replied with an easy smile.

Rousing himself, he turned his attention to the mute passenger that had come to the inn with them. He studied the Christmas tree in silence for a long moment, as if trying to decide the best way to approach the task ahead of him: getting the tree off the roof of his truck as well as the long bed, and up the steps, into the inn's main room.

Cris watched him regard the tree. It didn't take a clairvoyant to know what was going on in his mind. "You'll need help, you know," Cris told him.

The grin curving his mouth was lopsided. "Don't think I can handle a ten-foot tree by myself?" he asked.

She couldn't tell if he was being serious, but she knew what her honest answer had to be. "No. And it's closer to eleven feet tree than ten feet."

When he didn't respond immediately, she thought she'd insulted him, damaged his ego, but then Shane nodded.

"Smart lady," he pronounced. "Got any suggestions? I can't ask your father to help."

She said the first thing that came to mind. "I can pitch in."

He frowned. She couldn't be serious, could she? "No, you can't."

"Because I'm a girl?" she asked. She wouldn't have thought him guilty of that sort of prejudice, but that just proved she didn't know anyone as well as she thought she did.

"No," he replied, "because you're petite and delicate."

She looked surprised at his assessment. Obviously the man was paying closer attention to her than she figured. The thought warmed her. "I didn't think you'd noticed."

His eyes held hers for a long moment. "Oh, I noticed all right."

The next moment, they were no longer alone. Ricky had returned not only with his grandfather in tow, but two of his aunts and Wyatt, as well.

"See?" Ricky gestured at the tree proudly. "Isn't it beau-ti-ful?" he asked, expecting a chorus of agreement from the people he loved.

"Well, it certainly is big," Alex allowed. "But it's a little hard to tell if it's beautiful when it's tied up like that."

"First step is to get that baby down," Wyatt said, coming forward. "We'll need a knife to cut it free from the roof," he noted, surveying the way the tree had been tied.

"One knife coming up," Stevi volunteered, going back into the inn.

She returned in a few minutes, holding a long knife aloft. "Okay, let's get to it."

"Where did you get that knife?" Cris asked suspiciously.

"From my own personal knife collection," Stevi cracked. "What do you mean, where did I get it? From the kitchen, of course. Where else would I get a knife this big? Why? Do you have a special knife for cutting cords I don't know about?"

After taking the ten-inch knife from her sister, Cris examined it. "Just making sure it's not part of my boning set." It wasn't. "They're expensive," she explained.

Stevi shrugged. She still didn't see what the fuss was about. "A knife is a knife," she stated dismissively.

"Which is why you're the artist and I'm the inn's chef," Cris pointed out.

"You want me to go in and get another one?" Wyatt offered.

"No." She smiled her thanks. At least *someone* understood, she thought. "That one's all right to use," Cris told him.

It was all he needed to hear. Looking at Shane, Wyatt said, "Why don't you stand next to the top of the tree while I climb up and cut the base free from the roof?"

Shane nodded. "You got it." Anchoring the top of the tree by putting his weight on it, he said, "Okay, ready."

The ropes that Shane and the lot manager had used to secure the tree were thick enough to offer more than a little resistance. Cutting through them proved a more difficult challenge than either he or Wyatt were prepared for.

But by exercising patience, Wyatt managed to finally get through the braided ropes.

The second the ropes were cut away, the large blue spruce began to slide off the roof, gaining momentum as it did so. He, Shane, Cris and Richard all lunged for the runaway tree, grabbing any part of it they could.

Between them, they were able to keep the tree from falling completely off the truck and hitting the ground, but it came dangerously close to that before they regained control over it.

Muscles strained as they laid the runaway tree on the ground.

Wyatt started to cut the tree free of its remaining ropes, the ones holding the branches as flat as possible against the trunk.

"Leave the ropes in place," Shane instructed, stopping Wyatt. "They'll make it easier to carry the tree into the inn."

Wyatt stopped immediately and held the knife up to show that he'd heard Shane.

"Sorry," he apologized. "This is my first experience handling a real Christmas tree. Ours back home were always artificial."

He'd been overridden every year in his plea for a real tree. After a while, he'd stopped asking. Living on his own out in Hollywood, he hadn't bothered with Christmas decorations, thinking them wasted on just one person.

But this was different—and he was really looking forward to seeing the tree up and decorated. "My mother was afraid a real one might catch fire," he explained.

Ricky looked up at him with pity in his eyes, while Alex laughed. "Knew you were marrying me for a reason. You just wanted to be around a family with a real Christmas tree."

Wyatt lifted his hands in surrender. "You found me out. Guess the wedding's off, huh?"

"Over my dead body," Stevi informed the couple. "After everything I've gone through to pull this wedding together, you two are getting married even if you never speak another word to each other after the reception."

"That's our Stevi. Always the romantic," Cris said drolly.

Stevi glared at her. Because she was juggling Alex and Wyatt's wedding reception plans with her regular duties at the inn, as well as taking a few graduate art courses at the university, she was very irritable of late and it took little to set off her temper.

"Put a lid on it, Cris," she snapped.

"Put a lid on what?" Ricky asked, looking from Stevi to his mother. "I don't see a pot." He cocked his head as he regarded his aunt.

Alex patted his shoulder, diverting his attention and simultaneously defusing the situation as she shot Stevi a warning look.

"It's just an expression, honey," she told

the boy. "Aunt Stevi's a bit tense these days, but she's okay now. Right, Stevi?" she asked pointedly.

"Right. Sorry."

"Hey, a little help here," Wyatt urged. "Unless there's been a change in plans and we're going to decorate the Christmas tree out here, while it's on its side...."

"Might be worth considering," Alex said, feigning seriousness.

"I'll pretend I didn't hear that," Wyatt told her. Turning to Shane, he asked, "You ready?"

Rather than nod, because he was ready, Shane said, "Why not let me take that end? I'm taller."

Stepping back, Wyatt raised his hands as if surrendering. This wasn't about one-upmanship—it was about teamwork, and after being an only child, he, for one, was all for it.

"It's all yours," he told Shane.

"What can I do?" Cris asked. She hated just standing off to the side, watching Wyatt and Shane do all the work. Getting a free ride had never been her way. Cris liked pulling her own weight when it came to everything.

"Staying out of the way so we don't step on you jumps to mind," Wyatt told her.

He squatted and put his hands under the tree, all the while watching Shane, waiting for the other man's go-ahead.

"On the count of three," Shane said, bracing himself at the opposite end of the tree. When Wyatt nodded, Shane began to count, "One—two—"

"Three!" Alex declared, tackling the middle of the tree.

"Who told you to do that?" Wyatt demanded, on his feet, struggling to stabilize his end of the spruce.

"Haven't you heard?" Alex asked, doing her best not to pant. "I'm an emancipated woman. I don't have to wait for permission to do something. Now can we postpone this suffragette retro-debate and lug this tree inside before all three of us get hernias and have to put off the wedding—at which point Stevi will most likely kill us where we sleep."

"Convinces me," Wyatt declared, getting a slightly better grip on his end just before they all slowly made their way up the front steps.

"I'll grab the door!" Stevi volunteered, racing ahead to hold it open for them. She took a step back to be out of the way.

Cris was the only one facing forward at the time; the others were focused on the tree, which had turned out to be a lot heavier than they had expected. Because of her viewing advantage, Cris was the first to see a stunned Ms. Carlyle observing the impromptu parade as it moved into the inn with the bound-up tree.

Horrified at what she saw coming, Cris dashed madly into the inn, circumventing the others and just narrowly avoiding a collision with them.

"What are you doing?" Alex demanded. The next moment, she saw what her sister had anticipated happening. Cris had gotten to the former elementary schoolteacher in time to gently but firmly move the older woman aside so that she avoided a collision with the procession.

"Careful, Ms. Carlyle," Cris warned, once she had the elderly woman safely positioned.

"You don't want to be run over by a Christmas tree."

Ms. Carlyle sniffed. Very little in life managed to faze her these days. She took everything in stride, viewing it all with a grain of salt.

"For that to happen, my dear, the tree would have to come to life and be moving on its own power," the former teacher told her with a dismissive air. And then she inclined her head just the slightest bit. "But I thank you for your thoughtfulness, however misplaced," the woman acknowledged.

Cris flashed the woman a smile. She had a soft spot in her heart for the elderly woman, perhaps because Ms. Carlyle had no one, perhaps because she herself had never known her grandmother. "My pleasure."

"Where…?" Wyatt panted, looking around the immediate area.

Filling in the missing words, Alex knew Wyatt was asking her where she intended to have the tree standing.

"Here?" It wasn't a statement but more of a question directed toward her sister. She looked to Cris for validation of her choice.

"Make up your mind," Wyatt complained. "This thing is *heavy*."

"Here is good," Cris quickly agreed.

The moment that she did, Wyatt and Shane jointly placed the ever-heavier tree on the floor.

"I'm no expert when it comes to Christmas trees," Wyatt said as he looked at the tree he'd just put down, "but I'd say that we're going to need something to put the tree into."

"Dad?" Cris turned to her father. "Do you know where the—?"

"Christmas tree stand is?" he said, completing the question he'd anticipated his daughter asking. "Way ahead of you for once, Cris. I went looking for it the minute you left this morning to go tree hunting. It was in the rafters and I took it down." He faced his grandson. "Ricky, want to come with me to get the tree stand?"

Ponce de Leon's aide undoubtedly reacted the same way when asked to accompany the explorer in De Leon's search for the Fountain of Youth, Cris decided. "You bet!" the boy cried.

HALF AN HOUR later, the tree was upright, secured in the tree stand and actually standing straight—after half-a-dozen attempts to get it that way. All the ropes used to bind it had been cut off and now lay in pieces on the floor.

No one noticed that. What they all noticed was the tree and how majestic it appeared, even without any ornaments.

Alex summed it up for all of them when she said "Wow" in unabashed appreciation as she stepped back and took in the entire sight.

"See? Told ya it was a beau-ti-ful tree," Ricky exclaimed with no less enthusiasm than he'd demonstrated earlier. "Can we start decorating it now?" he asked, looking from his grandfather to his mother, hoping for a yes from one of them.

"What about the guests?" Wyatt asked, thinking some of them might want to join in the activity, as well.

Cris's mouth fell open. "Omigod, the guests! I forgot all about them," she lamented. A sense of urgency barreled through her veins. "I've got to get to the kitchen."

"Relax," Alex told her, grabbing her by the arm before she could take off. "I managed to catch Jorge before he left and Andy is in there now, helping him."

"Andy? *Our* Andy?" Cris cried. "Do we have the local ambulance on speed dial?"

"For your information," Alex said, "Andy has turned out to be quite the little cook, secretly taking a few cooking lessons on the side, she confessed. She pitched right in and, so far, none of the guests has keeled over or even complained of any stomach pains."

"Hey, the day's still young," Stevi cracked.

"Andy is doing just fine," Richard informed his second oldest. "Which means that you can go on doing what you were doing—unless you want to accompany me to get the decorations."

"Me, me," Ricky called, jumping up and down and waving his hand to get the man's attention. "I wanna get the decorations with you, Grandpa."

"I was already counting on that," Richard told him with a fond wink.

He put out his hand. Ricky slipped his into it and the two went off to the storage area. If anyone wanted to follow, the choice was theirs.

CHAPTER FIFTEEN

"ONE MORE, MAMA, just one more," Ricky begged between yawns. "Please?"

The "just one more" referred to his being allowed to hang up one more ornament since even *he* knew there was no way that the tree—*his* tree was how he thought of it—would be completely decorated in a single day, especially since the Christmas tree decorating had officially begun with more than half the day gone.

Ever since they'd gotten back with the trophy tree and had put it up, the joint effort to get all the lights on it had taken up a good deal of what was left of the day. A certain division of labor prevailed. Stevi was in charge of untangling the strings of lights that had somehow gotten mysteriously tangled in the eleven months since they had been put—supposedly neatly—away. Alex supervised which string of lights went where on

the tree, while Wyatt, Shane and Richard—
with the latter dealing strictly with the lower
third of the tree since that did not require
climbing a ladder—took over stringing the
multicolored tiny lights on the ten-foot-plus
blue spruce.

For sanity's sake, Ricky had been allowed
to sort the decorations with his mother. With
astonishing care, the boy took them out of
their boxes, put a hook through each of them
and laid the ornaments out on the large fold-
ing table Alex had brought out just for this
purpose. The ornaments were separated and
arranged by theme.

Despite the large number of existing ornaments, new ones found their way to the
tree every year. Almost all of those were
now coming from a popular greeting card
manufacturer and they had some sort of special significance attached to them for at least
one member of the family if not all of them.

Ricky was fondest of the "Baby's first
Christmas" ornaments, with both the year
of his birth and his name written on them.

There was also one framing his very first
photograph, taken at the hospital where he
was born, incorporated into the ornament.

Cris always saw to it that that particular one was the first ornament to be hung on the tree once the tree was ready for decoration. The beginning of the Christmas season didn't officially arrive until that ornament was hung in plain sight.

At this point, thanks to the enormous push from Wyatt and Shane, along with her father, the tree had on all its lights, but very few decorations beyond Ricky's tiny framed baby picture and two other ornaments that he favored, one from a science fiction movie he loved and one from a beloved cartoon bear, which was still his all-time favorite.

Cris looked down at the pleading face and felt herself giving in again, despite knowing she shouldn't. It was way past the boy's bedtime.

"You already begged for 'just one more' and I let you put up Silly-Billy, remember?"

"But if I don't put up any more tonight, they'll be all gone when I get up," Ricky pouted, gazing sorrowfully at the overloaded table of Christmas ornaments.

"No, they won't. I *promise* there'll be decorations for you to put up in the morning," Cris told the little boy.

Ricky's little eyelids were drooping and he was obviously losing his mighty battle to keep them open. But he didn't want to give in and trot off to bed yet because he really was afraid that somehow, the entire tree would wind up being completely decorated by the time he woke up in the morning.

Still, he was extremely tired and sinking fast.

"You promise?" he asked uncertainly, staring at his mother as much as he was capable of focusing at the moment.

"We both do," Shane said, adding his voice to the pledge. "As a matter of fact, if you want me to, I'll stand by the tree all night and make sure nobody hangs any of your special ornaments," he told the boy solemnly.

Ricky looked somewhat skeptical at Shane's offer, but there clearly wasn't a better one for him to consider, and it *was* getting harder and harder for him to keep his eyes open. All the energy he'd used up during the day had left him depleted.

"Is it a deal?" Shane asked, putting his hand out as if sealing a bargain with one of his adult customers.

There was absolutely nothing Ricky liked better than to be treated as an adult. So he put his small hand into Shane's and shook it just as heartily as he was able.

"Deal," he cried, following up the single word with yet another yawn.

That settled, Shane pretended to examine the little boy. "I'd say it was time to get you hustled off to bed. What do you say?"

"I'm not tired," Ricky protested with very little enthusiasm.

He rubbed one of his eyes as if to rub the sleep out of it. Instead, the action only seemed to reinforce his sleepiness.

"Of course you're not," Shane agreed wholeheartedly. "I'm just gonna pick you up and carry you off to bed in case we run into a stampede of dragons."

"Dragons?" Ricky mumbled, unable to muster even a little awe at the image of mythical dragons stampeding through the inn.

Dragons? Cris mouthed, gazing at Shane quizzically.

He shrugged good-naturedly. "First thing I could think of," he whispered back to her.

Grinning, Shane scooped the boy into his

arms and shifted his weight over to one side. Ricky didn't utter a word of protest. Instead, he just laid his head against Shane's shoulder. In less than thirty seconds, the boy's even breathing told Shane that Ricky had fallen asleep.

"Attaboy," Shane murmured, patting the small back reassuringly. Turning toward Cris, he said, "You want to lead the way to his room?"

In her opinion, Shane had done far more than enough for her and Ricky today. He'd gone above and beyond the call of duty more than twice over. He shouldn't have to put Ricky to bed, as well.

"Give him to me. I'll carry him to his room," she said, holding out her arms to Shane, waiting for the transfer.

But rather than transfer the boy to her, Shane kept his hand protectively on the boy's back.

"That's okay," he told her, keeping his voice low. "If I transfer him now, he might wake up. The less movement the better. Just show me which room is his."

As she walked from the main room, she saw Alex looking her way. The expression on her older sister's face all but shouted, *This one's a keeper, Cris. Grab him before he's gone.*

Or maybe that was just the refrain running perversely through her own brain, Cris thought.

She had to remind herself there was no reason for her to believe she would *ever* be in a position to "keep" anything, least of all a man like Shane. It was just her own loneliness making her think this way, a loneliness that cropped up in the middle of the night, when she sometimes lay awake by herself in her bed, remembering the way things had been when she and Mike had gotten married. The world had been fresh and new then, and so full of the promise of good things and happiness to come that she had felt immortal—and infinitely blessed.

She didn't know then how quickly things could change.

She did now, she once again acknowledged.

What she was doing, Cris thought as she went down the hall to the wing where her room and Ricky's room were located, was responding to kindness and allowing her mind to run wild. Shane was nothing if he was not very, very kind.

But that was his nature and she shouldn't allow herself to create baseless fantasies just because Shane was being his usual self.

Still, she couldn't help wondering, in a small, distant corridor of her mind, what it could be like if Shane was Ricky's father and she was Shane's wife.

Fantasy and speculation like that were for dreams in the night when she was asleep, not for taking up any of her waking hours, Cris silently castigated herself. She'd do well to remember that.

The problem was she really wasn't paying attention to her inner storm warnings.

Which was why she almost passed right by Ricky's room. Embarrassed, Cris quickly backtracked a couple of steps and then threw open her son's door.

"Right here," she said in a barely audible whisper, gesturing toward the bed as she walked in. "Just put him down right here and I'll get him ready for bed."

Shane eased the boy onto the bed. "Looks to me like he's already 'ready,'" he observed.

"I meant that I'll get him undressed and into his pajamas," Cris amended.

But as she reached out toward Ricky, Shane put his hand over hers with just enough pressure to still the movement. Cris looked up at him, quizzically raising one eyebrow even as she felt her heartbeat perversely increase.

"You start undressing him, he's liable to wake up again," Shane warned, "and these little guys can recharge their batteries in an instant. This tiny nap he's taking right now just might be all he needs to go another five hours."

"Five hours," she echoed, as if that was synonymous with her doing a stretch in purgatory. Cris banked a shudder.

Shane nodded. "If it were me, I wouldn't risk it just to get him to wear pajamas. When I was a kid, I did all my best sleeping in my street clothes," he told her with a grin. "As far as I'm concerned, wearing pajamas is highly overrated."

That sounded so silly to her—like something Ricky would suggest—she couldn't help laughing.

"Maybe you're right," Cris agreed. She

glanced back down at her son. He appeared so peaceful. She couldn't remember when she'd seen such a contented expression on his face. "Okay, I'll leave him in his play clothes. I just hope he doesn't think he can actually wear the clothes—especially his underwear—for two consecutive days."

Together they quietly left the room. "I can set him straight for you if you like," Shane offered once they were outside.

It would be one less thing for her to remember to do, she thought whimsically, even though she knew that in the end, she would handle this just as she handled everything that concerned her son.

Still, that didn't stop her from thanking Shane for his offer. "That would be very nice of you."

It wasn't any hardship on his part. "I get a kick out of the Ricky," he told her. "Spending time with him makes me think of what it might have been like if—if things had turned out differently," Shane concluded evasively.

He hadn't spelled it out, but she knew what Shane was thinking about without putting it into so many words. He was thinking about what it might have been like if his own child had lived. How simple things like going fishing or decorating a Christmas tree—or getting him to bed on time—might have shaped his own day-to-day life.

This much she could do for Shane: she could reassure him of something she felt in her bones. "As I said to you earlier, I *know* you would have made a really great father, given half a chance."

This time, instead of waving off her comment the way he'd done the last time, Shane smiled at her and said simply, "Thanks."

The single word, warmly uttered, corkscrewed its way into her very being, finding her heart as if it had a homing device implanted in it. The moment it did, she could feel her heart filling to capacity—even more—until it was close to bursting.

Rousing herself, she tried her best to maintain at least a small distance between them. Yes, he'd been wonderful to her son and, yes, he had been extremely helpful to her at every turn, but she couldn't allow that to melt her barriers or to get her thinking about a life that was forever closed off to her.

Besides, she had her former in-laws' impending visit to worry about. *That* should be the focus of her attention, if anything, since they should be here any time now.

Still, the nurturer within her refused to be silenced. At bottom, Cris supposed she was who she was and no set of circumstances would ever really change that.

Which was why she said to Shane, "It's late and you've put in a lot more than a full day. You look tired," she observed, working her way up to what she really wanted to propose. "Listen, instead of going all the way home, why don't you just stay over in one of the unoccupied rooms?" she suggested.

There had to be at least one that was unoccupied, she thought. The inn was rarely ever completely filled except on special occasions.

Or at least, that was what she recalled. Lately, she'd been so wrapped up in Ricky and her own little world, which rarely extended beyond the kitchen, that she was oblivious to everything that might be going on outside it.

The offer tempted Shane, but he never liked to be on the receiving end of special treatment. "I wouldn't want to impose."

"That's my line," she reminded him. "And yet, I keep imposing and you keep doing things for me you really have no reason to."

"At least none that seem obvious to you," Shane murmured.

His voice was so low she only picked up a couple of words—and neither one made any sense to her. "What?"

He hadn't really meant to say those words aloud, Shane thought ruefully. He was slipping, he chastised himself. "Nothing," he said, shaking his head. "Just mumbling."

"Mumble a little louder so I can hear, too," Cris urged, still waiting for him to clarify what he'd said—or at least repeat it more clearly.

"Just gibberish," he told her. "Wouldn't make any sense to you. Doesn't even make sense to me, really," he told her, covering his tracks.

"Okay, while you're decoding your gibberish, let me find out from Alex which room isn't occupied."

"You really don't have to do that," he called after her.

Cris pretended she didn't hear him and picked up her pace.

"Stay right there," she instructed, raising her voice as she looked over her shoulder. "I'll be right back."

"A ROOM?" ALEX asked, repeating her sister's request. "You want an unoccupied room?"

"Just for tonight," Cris emphasized. "Shane is really exhausted—even though he refuses to admit it—and he spent most of today humoring Ricky."

Alex smiled. She saw it just a bit differently. "And getting further entrenched on your good side."

Cris drew herself up, although she was far too tired herself to register indignation. "I don't have anything to do with it."

Alex shook her head. *None so blind as those who refuse to see.*

"You just keep telling yourself that," Alex said with a laugh. "In the meantime, here." Turning the old-fashioned ledger she had all the guests sign, she made it face Cris. "I've got a room for Shane. It's two doors down from Ms. Carlyle's suite. It's also just off the dining area," she said significantly. "You can peek out of the kitchen to see if he's there."

There was no use in Cris arguing that she

wouldn't be doing that. That they weren't an item the way Alex had already labeled them in her mind.

"Just give me the key," she requested coolly.

"Yes, ma'am." A half smile, half smirk played on Alex's lips as she handed Cris the keycard.

Cris hurried away without a word.

SHANE WAS EXACTLY where she'd left him.

She held out the keycard to him, telling him the number of the room.

Since he concentrated almost strictly on the area where he did his renovations and the area where he was now adding on a wing, the room number she told him was unfamiliar to him.

"Which way is that?"

"C'mon," she offered, "I'll show you."

"You don't have to," he said, falling into place beside her. He remembered to shorten his gait. "You can just point."

"I walk better than I point," she told him glibly.

Finding the room took no time at all. It passed, she silently lamented, *too* fast.

"See you tomorrow," she said once he'd opened the door with the keycard.

"Tomorrow," he repeated, wishing he could tell her that he didn't want tonight to end, that he enjoyed all the little things that had filled the day, like standing and talking to her, like hearing her laugh. Like breathing in the light scent of vanilla and honeysuckle that he had begun to associate with her.

Impulsively, Cris turned back toward him, said, "Thank you for everything," and brushed a quick kiss on his cheek before disappearing down the corridor.

He stood there awhile, looking after her even though she'd already disappeared from view.

"Ditto," he murmured, touching his cheek.

And then he went into his room.

CHAPTER SIXTEEN

BECAUSE OF THE noise factor and because the inn had many guests who felt no compulsion to compete with the roosters and wake up early, Shane could not begin work on either the renovations or the new wing until at least nine o'clock.

Which meant that Ricky was free to ambush the general contractor, who was always up early, and get Shane to continue decorating the Christmas tree with him. But the time to get the decorating done was tight because Ricky had to leave for kindergarten by eight. At best, Ricky and Shane had forty-five minutes in the morning to hang ornaments on the tall tree.

Because everyone at the inn doted on Cris's son, no one attempted to do any real decorating until Stevi brought him home from his kindergarten class at one o'clock.

Shane, who still wasn't in the habit of having a lunch break while on the job, did so for the entire week it took to turn the blue spruce tree into the heavily laden work of art that now stood like a bejeweled grand duchess in the center of the main room.

The decorating was slow going, but six days after the tree became part of the main room's decor, it was finally finished.

From everyone's viewpoint, the effort and the wait were well worth it.

This year's tree, Ricky announced with feeling, was the "best-est Christmas tree *ever.*"

"Pictures," Andy declared after the last ornament was hung and the family, for once, was all together. "We need to take pictures to commemorate this occasion."

So saying, Andy produced not only her trusty camera, which at times seemed almost like an extension of her, but her faithful tripod, as well. She began setting up the tripod immediately.

"Pictures?" Shane questioned, turning toward Cris for an explanation. She hadn't said anything about taking pictures.

"We do this every year," she explained.

And if he thought *this* was something, he

should be around on Christmas Eve when they officially opened their gifts. It occurred to her that having Shane around to share in their Christmas Eve celebration was definitely not without its appeal.

"Pictures are Andy's way of chronicling our lives together. We at least have photographs taken at approximately the same time each year to show how much we've grown or changed or something along those lines. All I know is that if we refuse, Andy becomes impossible to live with. Standing in front of the tree with smiles pasted on our faces is a small price to pay for peace and quiet," she assured him. Seeing his discomfort, she decided to come to his rescue, even though she would have welcomed commemorating his part in this year's Christmas activities. "You don't have to have your picture taken if you don't want to."

"Too late," he replied with a laugh as Ricky grabbed his hand and began pulling him into position next to him in front of the tree.

"Ricky—" Cris began, a warning note in her voice. It was one thing to commandeer one of his aunts or his grandfather—they were all putty in his hands anyway—but quite another to think he could do the same with someone who was just working at the inn.

Is that all Shane's doing? Just working at the inn? an annoying little voice in her head asked. With effort, she shut the voice out.

"It's okay, really," Shane assured her. He anticipated her reprimanding the little boy. "I don't mind."

She knew a lot of people who would balk at being taken over by a five-year-old. Shane's rating went up even higher in her book. He was already pretty highly rated. If this kept up, his rating would go through the roof, she thought with a smile she was completely unaware of.

But Shane wasn't.

"You are a very easygoing person," Cris commented out loud.

He gave her his philosophy in a nutshell— forged right after he'd lost his wife. "Life's too short not to be," Shane told her.

"Okay, everybody ready?" Andy asked, looking over her family members as Cris was practically pushed into place by her son.

Andy had even gone so far as to have

Wyatt locate Ms. Carlyle, who had done her part in the decorating by hanging several ornaments on the lower branches so she wouldn't have to exert herself in any fashion and could still feel part of the ceremony. The elderly woman had been included in each of the annual tree-decorating photographs ever since Andy had begun keeping an album dedicated to the tradition.

Having finally positioned her state-of-the-art camera on its tripod, Andy refrained from setting the timer until she was certain that everyone she wanted to include was in the room and within the immediate vicinity of the Christmas tree.

"Where's Ms. Carlyle?" she asked, looking around.

"Right here, Andrea," a gravelly voice informed her.

The woman had her arm threaded through Wyatt's and they were approaching the tree at a slow, steady pace. Ms. Carlyle was almost smiling. Almost, but not quite.

Although she had been aware of Wyatt, both boy and man, because of his stays at the inn, Ms. Carlyle hadn't actually had occasion to get to know him in any manner until he had conducted his extensive interviews with her about the inn's history. More than half the anecdotes in the book about all the various people, famous and not, who had passed through the inn's doors had come from Ms. Carlyle.

She was, and had always been, a great observer of people and their habits. She'd observed close to a thousand guests during their stays at the inn, including a number of Hollywood celebrities from what had come to be regarded as the movies' Golden Era.

Out of those interviews had grown a strong friendship and a mutual respect.

"You can't expect me to run," Ms. Carlyle was saying to Andy. Rather than cite her age as a factor, something she had never been known to do, Ms. Carlyle fell back on the teachings of etiquette. "Ladies never run," she informed Andy.

"Yes, ma'am," Andy agreed in a subdued voice that said she would never have dreamed of arguing with the woman. "I just wanted to be sure that Wyatt was bringing you here."

"I am bringing myself here, dear," Ms.

Carlyle corrected. "Wyatt is merely serving as my escort."

Andy inclined her head. "I stand corrected, Ms. Carlyle."

"No shame in that," the woman replied magnanimously. "One is never too old to keep learning. Now then," she said, and paused as she looked around at the array of familiar faces—all save the tall, strapping young man with the startlingly beautiful eyes. She had already made his acquaintance the first day he had come to work at the inn, but as far as she was concerned, Shane McCallister was very much the new boy on the block. "Where is it you would like me to stand?" she asked Andy politely.

"Somewhere in front of the tree would be perfect," Andy encouraged. "Wherever you'd like to stand will be fine. We'll all arrange ourselves around you once you're comfortable."

A delicate, incredulous laugh drifted through the air as Ms. Carlyle regarded her with amusement.

"My dear, I stopped being 'comfortable' as you so whimsically put it a good thirty years ago. The best one can hope for once one reaches my age is a lesser degree of discomfort."

Taking measured steps and attempting not to lean too heavily on the hand-carved, white-headed cane never far from her, Ms. Carlyle delicately positioned herself at the tree's center.

"Okay, everyone, gather around Ms. Carlyle," Andy encouraged, waving her family in to take positions on both sides of the retired elementary schoolteacher.

Ricky hadn't let go of Shane's hand, as though afraid that if he did, his new best friend would disappear. Tugging his hand now, Ricky took a place beside Ms. Carlyle, with Shane flanking his other side.

"Mama, stand next to Shane," he instructed like a small dictator.

"Yes, sir," Cris answered, executing a mock salute to her son.

Stevi slanted Cris a look. She was both amused and empathetic. "I think the sarcasm is lost on him. He's too young."

"What sarcasm?" Cris deadpanned. "I'm trying to stay on Ricky's good side. The way that boy is going, he'll be a mini-emperor by the time he's twelve. All he needs is his own country."

Pleased because he knew what an emperor was, Ricky giggled with pleasure.

"Clock's ticking, Andy," Cris prodded as Andy checked a few things while looking through the viewfinder. "Some of us actually have to work for a living and we need to get back to it," she teased her kid sister.

"Almost ready," Andy promised, adjusting some of the settings at the last minute. "Ready," she announced. She pushed the timer and made a beeline for the perimeter of the gathered group. Releasing a long breath, she faced forward and instructed, "Okay, everyone, say cheese."

"Four years in college for a degree in fine arts with an emphasis on photography and 'say cheese' is the best you can come up with?" Stevi asked, feigning wonder.

"How about 'say Camembert'?" Andy cracked.

"One need not say anything," Ms. Carlyle interjected. She was being unusually loquacious, Cris noticed, wondering with affection what had set the woman off. "One need only hold back one's smile until the proper moment, such as now."

The tiniest hint of a smile curved the woman's small mouth just as the timer went off, causing the camera shutter to click and a small flash to go off. "Well, another year commemorated," Ms. Carlyle said, beginning to move away from the group.

Andy held up her hand. "Wait. One more photograph for luck," she reminded the woman, all but begging.

"Ah, yes, the 'lucky' photograph that is always identical to the one that came before it." With a resigned sigh, Ms. Carlyle got back into position and held herself the exact same way she had previously, with her back ramrod straight. "Set the timer, Andrea," the woman instructed.

Ricky wasn't the only dictator in the group, Cris couldn't help thinking, glancing toward Shane to see how he was holding up.

"Eyes front, Cris," Andy ordered, pressing the appropriate button and then dashing back to the group and her position.

This time the flash went off just as she was turning around. Andy looked dismayed and frustrated.

"Something different," Cris said with an encouraging smile as she assessed the situation.

"A spontaneous, live-action shot," Wyatt told his future sister-in-law, adding his two cents. "Those always end up the best," he assured Andy before turning back to Ms. Carlyle. "May I escort you back to the veranda?" he suggested since that was where he'd found her sitting when he'd been dispatched to bring her to the main room for the photograph.

"I've gotten enough sun today. Don't want to look too tanned. Nothing worse than appearing like one of those poor, misguided young women who think that darkening their skin and partying hard is the proper way to live.

"'Beauty is as beauty does,' is not just something to stitch on a pillow. It still means as much these days as in Ben Franklin's when he was writing *Poor Richard's Almanack*."

Doing his best to follow what was being said, and hearing his grandfather's name mentioned, Ricky looked from the elderly woman to his grandfather. "Are you poor,

Grandpa?" He had never thought of his family in those terms.

"Not when I have you, your mother and your aunts in my life," Richard responded with a wide smile. "Taking all that into consideration, I'd say I was one of the richest men around."

In response to the last words, Ricky's eyes lit up. "Grandpa, I saw this really neat bicycle on TV," Ricky began.

"Really walked into that one, Dad." Alex laughed.

"What kind of a bicycle?" Wyatt wanted to know, pausing a moment before escorting Ms. Carlyle to wherever she felt like going.

"Don't you dare," Cris warned. "The tricycle Ricky has now is just fine."

"What's money if you can't use it to spoil your nephew once in a while?" Wyatt asked, ruffling Ricky's hair.

"Yeah, Mama," Ricky piped up. "What's money if you can't spend it that way?"

She supposed it was never too early for a lesson in practicality. She didn't want her son to grow up to be one of those men who thought that the world owed him something. He needed to know that most people worked hard for their money, not just had it rain down on them every time they wanted it. A man could easily lose his self-respect that way.

"It's something you save so that when you need it for important things, it's there."

"Bicycles are important," Ricky told her with complete sincerity.

There was no talking him out of it now, she thought. It would be best to resume this discussion at another time. "We'll talk about this later," Cris informed her son crisply. "Right now, I've got lunches to get ready for our guests."

"Sorry," Wyatt apologized. "I guess I just get carried away a little."

"You meant well," Cris acknowledged, softening toward her future brother-in-law. "And it's hard not to give in to Ricky and spoil him when he's the only child in the family."

Wyatt laced his fingers through Alex's and said, "We'll see what we can do about that after the wedding."

"Wyatt," Alex chided, embarrassed.

Shane took that to mean it was his presence that had embarrassed her, since everyone else in the room—even Ms. Carlyle—was considered family.

"I'd better get back to work, too," he said, addressing the gathering in general. "I've got a crew coming in next week to help put up the plasterboard and they won't be able to put up anything if I don't have the area ready for them."

He turned just as an older, exceptionally well-dressed couple walked in through the front door. Their refined apparel made them look out of place in a mostly beach atmosphere. But what set them apart for Shane was the couple's almost palpable aloofness.

Who *were* these people?

Cris found her tongue first. Taking a deep breath, trying to will away the numbness that had set into her limbs, she forced herself to step forward. "Mr. and Mrs. MacDonald, you're here."

"Don't look so surprised, I did leave you a message," Marion MacDonald said to her coolly. "I assumed you checked your messages."

"Yes, I checked," Cris answered, feeling herself losing ground right on the spot.

"Your message said you were coming within a week."

"Well, dear, unless I've forgotten how to read a calendar, this *is* within a week." The woman smiled a smile that never reached her eyes, which narrowed as she focused on her former daughter-in-law.

"We've come to have that talk, Cristina."

CHAPTER SEVENTEEN

ALTHOUGH EXPECTED, the arrival of Cris's former in-laws *still* managed to stun them all.

But as reality sank in, Richard stepped forward, sincerely hoping that whatever had prompted this trip to San Diego and his inn could be dealt with, with common sense and civility.

He wore his very best innkeeper/unofficial mediator smile. "Why don't we get you settled in first and then we can all talk and catch up?"

Marion MacDonald raised her ice-blue eyes to his and fixed the man before her with what seemed to Shane a barely veiled look of superiority.

Though the woman and her husband had met Cris's father at Mike's funeral, she regarded him now without a trace of recognition.

"I'm sorry," she said formally, "and you are?"

"Richard Roman," Richard replied, taking no offense at her unconscious snub. "We met at Mike's funeral. This is my inn and Cris is my daughter," he told her.

It was both an introduction and a warning. Though he was an incredibly friendly man given to being low-key, he was not about to tolerate rude or condescending behavior toward any member of his family, intended or otherwise. From what Cris had told him, Mike's parents behaved as though they belonged to the privileged class, a class he and his family were clearly not a part of. He had a feeling that at best, he and his family were politely tolerated.

"That's very thoughtful of you, Richard," Marion replied. "However, there is no need for either of us to 'settle in.'" She repeated Richard's words with disdain, as if he had used a quaint regionalism. "Arthur and I are actually staying in a suite at the Hilton."

"We would gladly have put you up here," Richard told her, indicating there was no need to pay for accommodations some distance away when the MacDonalds could just as easily have stayed at the inn free.

"Yes, well, we've already checked in there and are quite comfortable, thank you. There would be no point in uprooting and coming here. We won't be staying that long. Just long enough to have a few words with your lovely daughter here." She said the words without feeling, as if she knew that some sort of compliment was expected and she was living up to her part of the social covenant.

Cris shifted uncomfortably. The woman was as cold and distant as she'd always been, Cris thought. Instinctively, she placed her hand protectively on her son's shoulder.

Stomach tightening, nerves almost at the point of snapping, Cris couldn't stand not knowing any longer. "Exactly what is it about Ricky's future that you want to discuss?" she asked, trying her best not to let fear enter her voice.

She could see that Mike's mother took the question as a challenge to her authority. Cris hadn't meant it that way, but she knew that if she continued being mild mannered, Marion would see that as weakness and walk all over her.

If she were the only one involved, maybe she would have allowed it.

But there was Ricky to think of and she wasn't about to have her son go through what Mike had confided *he* had endured at that age.

Although it was obvious the woman neither liked being questioned nor cared for having to explain herself in any fashion, apparently to keep matters civil she made an effort to smooth things out just a little. "His education," Marion said, answering Cris's question. "Richard will be starting first grade in the fall and we—Arthur and I—have certain ideas about where Richard should go."

Cris had named the boy after her father, but no one had called him by his full name since he'd been baptized, and even then, only on that one occasion.

"He prefers to be called Ricky," Cris informed the woman as she closed her arms around the boy while never taking her eyes off Marion.

The woman seemed unwilling even to repeat the nickname. "Yes, well, he'll grow out of that. A year at the San Francisco Boys Academy will see to that, among other things," she told Cris in no uncertain terms.

"Definitely," Arthur agreed in a raspy voice.

Cris looked from one to the other, stunned. What were they talking about? "Excuse me?"

This had all the signs of turning ugly, Richard decided. "Stevi, why don't you take Ricky outside to play a little?" Richard suggested.

Stevi was about to protest her father's request, pointing out that it was getting dark, but then she realized why she was being dispatched with the boy. Stevi put her hand out for Ricky's.

"C'mon, I need to show you something outside," Stevi coaxed.

The expression on the boy's face clearly indicated he was torn between his desire to play outside at night—a rare treat—and remain here, listening to the adults talk. There were moments when Cris thought her son had an old soul. He had the ability to fit right in with people four times his age.

But not at this moment.

The second Ricky allowed himself to be led off, Cris picked up the conversation where she'd dropped it.

"Just what are you talking about, Marion?" Cris demanded, tapping into courage she hadn't realized she had. "Ricky isn't going to any academy."

"Oh, but he must. You don't expect him to go to a *public* school, do you?" As far as the woman was concerned, it was a rhetorical question.

She wasn't prepared to hear Cris say, "That's exactly what I expect. His kindergarten has a very fine school attached to it."

"Yes, well, perhaps for the children in the area, but Richard is a MacDonald. There are certain expectations he'll have to live up to," Marion pointed out.

"The only expectation he has to live up to is to be a good, decent human being," Cris said.

"Oh, my dear, you have *so* much to learn," the woman said, laughing and shaking her head.

"Maybe," Cris allowed. "But not about

Ricky. I'm his mother and I know what's best for my son."

There was contempt in the older woman's eyes. "Apparently not. Arthur and I can give him things you can't, provide him with opportunities you would never be able to provide him with. You can't seriously want to deny him the world we can introduce him to."

Had Mike not told her how lonely he'd been, how unloved he'd felt in this world Marion was talking about, she might have been induced to put her heart aside and give Ricky to these people. But Mike *had* told her and she was convinced that love trumped money every time.

"I can, and I do," Cris replied. "I'm not giving you my son. He doesn't even *know* you."

Marion looked at her as if she was spouting gibberish. "What does that have to do with my proposal?" she demanded.

"That's my whole point," Cris cried. "It has *everything* to do with it."

"Young woman, you're talking nonsense. I am talking about giving Richard the world on a platter and you are talking about—well,

I don't know *what* you're talking about. All I know is that you are trying to deprive my grandson." Marion took a breath, then, before anyone else could say anything, she tried another approach. "Look, be reasonable. I'm sure you can see that Arthur and I can provide far better for our grandson than you, with your meager funds and abilities, could ever dream of doing. We can give him all the creature comforts he'd ever possibly want, introduce him to the finer things in life. What can you do for him? Train him to be a bellhop?"

Out of the corner of her eye, Cris saw Alex struggling not to tell the woman off. Cris deliberately waved her back. "*Ricky* doesn't need creature comforts. What my son needs is love—something that was, according to Mike, and most likely still is, in extremely short supply in your museum of a house." Fighting to keep her fraying temper in check, she told the couple, "If you aren't here to spend the holidays with your grandson or begin building some sort of decent relationship with Ricky, I suggest you go back to where you came from. Now," she concluded with emphasis.

Marion's carefully made-up face turned ugly right before Cris's eyes. "We'll go for the moment, but we are *not* leaving San Diego without the boy. I'm afraid you leave us no choice. If we cannot make you see that this is in the boy's best interest, then we will have to file for sole custody of Richard."

Alex could not stand it anymore. "Why?" she demanded, moving forward. Her very stance was confrontational. "It can't be because you love him. If you did, you'd leave him with his mother."

"For your information, we have *tried* to get your sister to move into our house, but she refused. Twice," Arthur underscored, speaking up at last. "We understand that she's attached to this place, but we have an obligation to make sure our son's boy is raised properly."

Cris clenched her hands into fists at her sides, fervently wishing she could take a swing at each MacDonald. But that would only give them ammunition to have her declared an unfit mother. So all she could do was repeat, "He's not going with you."

The steely look on Marion's face said she was confident they had already won the battle and there were merely some formalities to go through. "If you choose to fight us on this, we *will* take you to court—and you *will* lose. If you like, we can just, say, make a sizable donation to the inn in exchange for your cooperation in this matter."

"This 'matter' is her son," Shane interjected, surprising the others. "She's the boy's mother." He'd tried to hold on to his temper as long as possible, feeling it wasn't his place to say anything. But he couldn't stand by and watch Cris being bullied this way. "Mothers are awarded custody of their children all over the country."

"Perhaps in general," Marion allowed, then gave them all a preview of how the case would go. She had come prepared. "But she is a *single* mother, working in a dead-end job at a quaint motel that has trouble staying in the black. We've done our research, you see—just in case," she told Cris. "We, the boy's grandparents, on the other hand, are quite well-to-do and well regarded in the upper circles of society. What that means in simple terms is that we have the money to keep fighting this until we win."

Marion delivered her summation fully expecting to overwhelm the woman her son had so irresponsibly selected as a mate.

"Be reasonable, Cristina. We *can* give Richard everything. By your own admission, all you can give him is love—which wears thin after a while. If you were to keep him, as he grows up—doing without so many things—he will resent you for it," Marion predicted solemnly.

But Cris could only shake her head. "You don't know the first thing about raising a child," she told the couple, and there was actually a touch of pity in her voice because clearly they *couldn't* see. "Ricky will resent me if I give him up without a fight."

"Then by all means, fight for him—a little," Arthur counseled, about to offer what was obviously a compromise. "Make a show of it—then be gracious and step away. We all want the best for the boy and only one side can provide that for him. Be smart. Accept the money, leave the boy. You'll both prosper," he concluded with a smile.

His wife took the lead again, striking what in their estimation should have been the victory blow. "Now this can go peacefully, and the boy will be left without scars.

Or it can be dragged out in the courtroom, where Richard will be subjected to rigorous cross-examination and an experience he will not look back on with fondness. He will grow to hate you for the turmoil in his life as well as for keeping him away from the finer things—because we *will* win. If you are truly interested in his welfare, step away. Otherwise, this court battle *will* hurt him," Marion emphasized.

"If anything, we have been far too complacent about this situation far too long. Richard," Arthur stressed, adding his voice to Marion's argument, "is our main concern and we are not about to give him up."

"And neither am I," Cris informed her former in-laws firmly. Nothing they said would change her mind. In her heart, she knew she was right—knew Mike would have agreed with her.

Richard had had enough. As a rule, he tried hard to keep out of his daughters' lives, but this was asking too much of him. He loved Ricky and would do everything in his power to make the boy happy—and that meant keeping him in a loving home.

"Under the circumstances," he said to the

couple, "I trust you'll understand if I ask you to leave my inn."

"Oh, completely," Marion agreed. "And we leave with pleasure. But this matter is far from over and you *will* be hearing from our lawyer," she told Cris before she walked regally out the front door with her husband following a step behind.

"Well, there's one woman who won't have to worry about being picked for Mother of the Year," Alex muttered, but loud enough for everyone to hear.

Cris laughed, yet she felt very shaky. Mike's parents could *buy* a judge if they had to. This was far worse than she had anticipated.

"Was she always like that?" Andy asked her.

"Mike didn't talk about his childhood much," Cris said, answering her, "but the little he did say gave me the impression she was never really a mother to him in the real sense of the word. She was more like the empress who ruled over the kingdom. The only time she showed any interest in him was when he did something she felt would embarrass her. She was furious when she found out he'd enlisted 'like a common blue-collar underachiever,'" Cris said, quoting what Mike had told her. The memory made her even angrier.

"I sure hope he did things that embarrassed her a lot," Alex said with feeling.

"Everything's going to be all right," Wyatt promised as he took out his cell phone.

Alex moved closer to him, glancing at the phone to see the number Wyatt was keying in. "Who are you calling?"

Wyatt finished tapping numbers on the keypad. "This lawyer I know in L.A. He's got an excellent track record and he's as sharp as they come."

"Does he mind being paid on the installment plan?" Cris asked.

She had some money set aside, initially started for Ricky's college fund. However, there wasn't all that much accumulated and she *knew* it wouldn't be enough to cover the expense of a high-powered lawyer—which, she had a feeling, she would need if she had a prayer of winning against the MacDonalds.

"He owes me a favor," Wyatt told her. "Don't worry about it. You'll need the best if those two are really going to go through with their threat about taking you to court."

Cris was in shock. None of this was making any sense to her. She shouldn't have to fight for Ricky. She had always put his needs ahead of her own. Why was this happening?

"But I'm his mother," she cried. "And they're two cold-blooded, self-absorbed people who don't know the first thing about making a child feel secure and happy." She looked at Wyatt. "Could they win just because they're rich?" she demanded.

"I'd like to say no, but anything is possible," Wyatt told her honestly. "Your being a single mother doesn't exactly strengthen your position. They'll point out that you're too busy working to watch after Ricky—"

"But there's always someone here for him when I am busy," she protested.

"They'll be dismissive and say that indicates an unstable atmosphere—he never knows who he'll be with," Wyatt told her, playing devil's advocate.

"Family. He's always with family," Cris emphasized, her voice cracking.

She was getting too emotional, she told herself. That led to making mistakes.

Breathe in, breathe out. Center, she silently ordered, her eyes shut tight.

What Wyatt said next made them fly open.

"They'll do everything they can to dig up some dirt on you—"

"I have no dirt," Cris protested indignantly. "I'm as boringly spotless as they come." To illustrate her point, she said, "Mike was the only man I've ever been with and that was *after* we got married. Like I said, in the MacDonalds' world, I'm certifiably boring."

"How about after Mike died?" Wyatt asked. "Was there anyone then?"

Cris shook her head. "Not really. I went out on a couple of dates with this one guy who turned out not to be worth my time."

Wyatt paused for a second, as if searching for a delicate way to ask the next question. "Anything happen with him?"

Cris knew what he was after. "Yes," she answered honestly. "His ego was broken."

"Can he be bought?" Shane asked, speaking up suddenly.

She'd gotten so wrapped up in the possibility of having to fight for Ricky she'd completely forgotten that Shane was in the room. She wasn't sure what he was asking.

"What?"

"This guy you went out with," Shane said. "Can he be bought?"

"I still don't understand," Cris told him, feeling a little thickheaded.

Of course she didn't understand, Shane mused. Because she was too nice, because she would have never thought of doing something like that herself. He would have bet his soul that no matter what, Cris would never lie for money.

"Can your former in-laws buy this guy off, give him money to say that you slept with him—as well as with his friends. Lies like that," Shane elaborated. He watched the light all but go out of her eyes. He hadn't wanted to say those things, but she had to understand the type of people she would find herself up against.

"No," Cris cried with feeling, and then she reexamined her response. Carefully. The truth of it was she couldn't be adamant about her response. She didn't know the man nearly well enough to bet the outcome in a custody battle on his integrity. She shook her head. "I honestly don't know," she admitted. And then, though it hurt and frightened her to the point of near panic, she said, "Maybe."

"Have you been in contact with him since you dated?" Shane asked.

Cris shook her head. "Absolutely not. To be honest, after that experience left a bad taste in my mouth, I didn't really want to have anything to do with him at all. For all I know, he's left the area. I heard via the grapevine that he got laid off from his job, so maybe he relocated elsewhere."

She was grasping at straws and she knew it. But she had never felt this frightened, not even when she had found out that Mike had been killed, with her about to give birth to his child.

"You know," Wyatt said thoughtfully, "with your spotless record, things would be completely in your corner if you were just married."

Well, that wasn't going to happen, Cris thought, so there was no purpose in talking about it. "Or if I was a mermaid and I could grab Ricky and swim away from here with Ricky riding on my back."

"I think getting a husband might be easier than growing a fish tail," Shane theorized.

Humor. Right now she didn't need humor, she thought. What she needed was a solution—or, barring that, some sort of an escape plan.

"And exactly how would I go about getting this husband? Advertise for one in the newspaper, or just get on social media and say 'I'd like one husband, please. Doing chores not required, no expertise necessary. Must be able to stand and look manly when so-called wife deals with fire-breathing former in-laws.'"

She slanted a look at Shane. "Sounds like a piece of cake to me. How about you? Does it sound like a piece of cake to you? Or do you know something I don't about locating a man willing to stand in?"

"Not sure I understand what you mean by stand in," Shane said, "but I'd be willing."

"Willing?" she echoed, confused as to his meaning. "Willing to what?"

"Willing to marry you so you could retain custody of Ricky."

CHAPTER EIGHTEEN

RICHARD WAS THE first to find his voice. Rather than dismiss the offer out of hand, as Cris thought he would, her father asked Shane, "Young man, are you serious?"

Turning toward Shane, she half expected him to laugh and say he'd just made a very poor joke.

But he didn't.

Instead, in a calm, collected voice, Shane said to her father, "I've never been more serious in my life, sir."

It was Alex who showed the first emotion. "This isn't some game show, or a half-baked reality program, Shane," her sister informed him, barely suppressed anger flashing in her eyes, not at him but at the people who had just left. "Those horrible people who just walked out of here are dead serious. They want custody of Ricky. If you go through with this charade, you'll have to go through it all the way," she warned Shane, "and they have the money to hire not just the best lawyers, but the best private investigators, as well."

"Private investigators?" Stevi echoed, walking back in with Ricky. She looked from one member of her family to another for answers. "Who's getting private investigators?"

"The MacDonalds, most likely," Cris spoke up, weary and exasperated at the same time. She'd *known* she would pay a price for being so content, so happy. Once again she banked a wild desire to grab Ricky and start running as fast and for as long as she could.

"Why would they want private investigators?" Stevi wanted to know, not quite following the logic of what was happening.

"To examine everything about my life. And yours," Cris said, suddenly turning to face Shane. If, by some wild chance, she became desperate enough to accept his offer, that would be what he would be up against. "Under a microscope, shred by tiny shred. If you borrowed someone's crayon in the first grade and forgot to give it back, they'll find out and twist it so that you come out looking like a criminal." She shook her head. It wasn't going to work. He needed to keep away from her before the MacDonalds ruined his life the way they'd almost ruined Mike's. "You don't want to get mixed up in something like this, Shane," she told him.

Rather than take the opening she'd just handed him, he laughed.

"See, you're sounding like a wife already, telling me what I want and what I don't want." The small smile on his lips receded. "No offense, Cris, but only I know what I want to do and what I don't want to do." And he wouldn't have offered, he thought, if he hadn't wanted to go through with it.

Ricky wriggled in between the adults. "Mama, look what my other grandpa just gave me." He proudly held up a bill for her to see. A crisp Benjamin Franklin. The attempt to buy her son's affections had started already, she thought. "He said I could keep it. Can I, Mama?"

Cris pressed her lips together and forced herself to think before she spoke. She looked accusingly at Stevi, who shrugged helplessly. "I tried to stop him—Mike's dad insisted

Ricky keep it. I didn't see the harm—I'm sorry."

"Not your fault." Cris closed her eyes for a moment to keep back angry tears. "It shouldn't surprise me that Arthur's trying to buy Ricky outright."

Ricky, meanwhile, had made his way over to Richard. Planting himself in front of his one true "grandpa," Ricky offered the hundred-dollar bill to him. "Here, Grandpa. I want to help. This is so you can pay for Aunt Alex's wedding."

Looking on, Shane was moved. "Nobody's buying this kid, Cris," he told Cris. "You raised that boy right."

"I'll mortgage the inn, Cris," Richard told his daughter with feeling. "Nobody's taking Ricky away from here."

This was the first the little boy had really heard why his grandparents had come to the inn. "Somebody wants to take me away?" Ricky cried, fear and confusion registering on his small face.

"Your other grandparents," Wyatt told him gently as he studied Ricky's expression. "Do you like those people who were just here, Ricky?" he asked casually, still studying the boy's face.

The slim shoulders rose and fell. "They're okay, I guess. They don't talk much," he confided in a lower voice.

"How would you feel about living with them for a while?" Wyatt wanted to know. The next moment, Alex elbowed him in the ribs. Hard.

He ignored her and waited to see Ricky's reaction to gauge what they were up against.

The question had been lightly tendered, but it wasn't received that way. Ricky's eyes instantly widened and mounting fear was evident in them. Exactly what Cris had always tried so hard to keep *out* of Ricky's life.

Ricky looked at his mother, the person who always had an answer to any question he came up with. And now she was going to give him to those other grandparents?

"Don't you love me anymore?"

"Oh, Lord, Ricky," she cried, dropping to her knees and hugging the boy. "I love you more than life itself."

"Every last dime, Cris," Richard echoed, speaking up again as he fought back tears at his grandson's question. The MacDonalds had no right to pull apart his family like this just because they were rich. "Whatever it takes to keep Ricky right where he is, I'll do it," he promised.

"I can get a part-time job at the art gallery," Stevi volunteered. "Maybe even talk them into hiring me full-time. I'll turn all the checks over to you so we can get some big-time lawyer to teach those people a lesson," she concluded with relish.

"I already told you that you don't have to worry about the cost of the lawyer," Wyatt reminded them. "That'll all be attended to."

She didn't want to owe anyone anything, even family. And she definitely didn't want Wyatt put in an awkward position because of her.

"What if he doesn't feel he 'owes' you," Cris wanted to know. "Then what?"

Wyatt shrugged. He was the screenwriter of a number of successful movies. When Hollywood smiled upon someone, the rewards were more than substantial.

"Then I'll owe him," he told Cris. "Either way, you don't have to worry."

"I've got some money saved up," Alex told

Cris, interrupting Wyatt. She took hold of Cris's hands. They were ice-cold, she noted. "It's all yours—you know that, right?"

Cris was getting really choked up. Everyone was standing with her in this awful, awful time. She didn't want them getting pulled into the matter. Mike had told her his mother's wrath could be horrible when fully aroused.

Cris didn't want the MacDonalds to have an excuse to come after her family— "My offer is still on the table," Shane told her quietly, breaking into her thoughts. A small smile curved the corners of his mouth as he added, "With no strings attached."

Cris looked at him, not certain what to make of the offer, knowing only that she felt entirely and emotionally overwhelmed.

"Didn't they call that a marriage of convenience in your day, Dad?" Alex asked, turning toward her father.

"I don't know. In 'my day' they'd just barely invented marriage," Richard cracked, attempting to get a smile out of Cris. She tried, but she just couldn't manage the effort. Richard put his arm around her shoulders and gave her a warm hug. "It's going to be all right, Cris, I promise."

No, it wasn't, she thought. *Maybe it would never be all right again.*

Cris covered her mouth to keep back a sob, then suddenly ran from the main room and out the front door. She kept on running, down the front steps and then around the side of the inn.

She stopped there. Leaning against the building, she struggled to get herself under control and keep the hot tears from spilling out.

She wasn't all that successful.

"Pretending to be married to me is that off-putting?" the deep male voice behind queried.

It was all Cris could do not to jump five inches off the ground, until she realized who it was.

She hadn't heard Shane come up behind her. Hadn't heard anything but the pounding of her heart as she tried desperately to deal with the situation and somehow put it into perspective.

"Of course not," she answered Shane. "But I can't have you do that. I can't be responsible for everyone sacrificing so much for me," she cried. The guilt was enormous.

"Did it ever occur to you," he asked, beginning slowly, "that they're doing it for themselves as much as for you?" He saw bewilderment in her eyes. "The way they all see it, they're doing whatever is in their power not to have their family torn apart by that woman and her husband. Doesn't take a brain surgeon to see what everyone thinks of your former in-laws. Those very same people are crazy about Ricky—as well as you."

She inclined her head, not finding anything to disagree with him about. "That explains why they're doing it." Her eyes met his. "But not why you are."

"Maybe it does," he told her quietly. He could see that she still didn't understand. "Maybe I want to help any way I can, too. And maybe, just maybe, I want to have the chance to say, even if it's only temporary and only make-believe, that I'm married to one of the kindest, most beautiful women I've ever met."

There went the corners of her eyes, she thought in exasperation. Leaking.

The next moment, in complete silence,

Shane dug into his pocket and found his handkerchief. He presented it to her without a word. She accepted it in kind and wiped her eyes.

"Thanks," she finally whispered hoarsely.

Cris pressed her lips together, really overwhelmed. And sorely tempted to take Shane up on his offer. It would make things so much easier, and right now she could certainly do with a wagonload of "easier."

She pulled in a deep breath as she looked around, trying to gather her thoughts. Wishing she had some sort of a sign telling her what to do, what would be the *right* thing to do.

That was when she happened to glance at her mother's azalea bush.

And her heart stopped for a second as what she was looking at registered.

"It's blooming like crazy," she said in a hushed voice, more to herself than to Shane.

"What is?" he asked. Was saying something out of left field Cris's way of diverting him from the subject?

"The azalea bush." Cris pointed straight at it. "Mama's azalea bush, it's blooming."

"And it's not supposed to at this time of

year?" he asked. He didn't know the first thing about plants, much less what they were called or what they were supposed to do. But judging by the look on Cris's face, this was an event worth noting.

"Not right now," she replied, still staring at the bush in wonder.

Maybe this was the omen she was looking for, Cris thought. Maybe this was a sign that she was supposed to take Shane up on his offer.

Or was she just grasping at straws?

As she looked at Shane, it occurred to her that he probably didn't know about the bush and most likely thought she had lost her mind and was babbling.

So she told him the story behind the azalea bush.

"The day of my mother's funeral, someone gave my father a potted azalea plant. Silvio, our gardener, planted it in the garden on this side of the inn the same day within view of the porch. He remembered that my mother liked to sit on the porch at night.

"The azalea blooms almost all year-round," she went on. "When Uncle Dan, Wyatt's dad, died, the bush suddenly looked like it was fading. It died back and we thought it was all over for the bush. But when Wyatt asked Alex to marry him and she said yes, the azalea exploded with blossoms." Her mouth curved in a fond smile, connecting to a faraway yesterday. "Dad likes to say that was Mama's way of showing how she felt about something. In this case, it's how she feels about Alex and Wyatt getting married. I might be crazy, but it looks as if it's suddenly blooming again. I didn't even notice it when I came out here—not until you commented." Maybe it was just wishful thinking on her part. Maybe she was just seeing what she *wanted* to see.

But she couldn't convince herself that she was just imagining it.

Shane was willing to go along with the myth of the azalea bush. He'd never been a skeptic about things his intellect could not sort out.

"Well," Shane drawled, "I'm no expert but maybe it *is* your mother, letting you know she thinks what I suggested is a good idea." He grinned at her nonchalantly, yet somehow it seemed extremely intimate. He had it all worked out. He was nothing if not de-tail oriented. "We can fly to Vegas, get married and be back by tomorrow night. Maybe even in time for you to make dinner for the guests," he speculated, knowing how wedded she was to her schedules.

Cris was still vacillating. "I feel terrible—"

"Not something a man wants to hear when he proposes marriage," he pointed out.

"A marriage in name only," she reminded him. "You're doing all this for me and I'm not doing anything for you in return."

"Now there you're wrong," he contradicted. "Being around you and Ricky and the rest of your family reminded me what it felt like to belong, to have people around who cared if you lived or died—who cared if you showed up in the morning."

There was gratitude in his eyes as he told her, "I've felt more alive these past few weeks, working on your family's inn, than I have since my wife died. I figured there was no way I could pay you back for that—but now there is. I can do something to help you keep your own little family unit together. And those private investigators you were worried about—"

He had her attention. "Yes?"

"They're going to be very disappointed and very bored. I didn't even borrow that hypothetical crayon you mentioned earlier. I was so honorable that I didn't even tell a girl in high school how I felt about her because she was going with this guy she was crazy about and I didn't want to spoil it for her."

"So you never told her?" she asked incredulously.

He looked at her for a long moment before shaking his head slowly and answering. "No."

"What happened to her?" Cris wanted to know, her eyes never leaving his. Something about the story had struck a nerve.

"She married the other guy," he answered in an unsettlingly low voice.

Something wouldn't allow her to let the story he'd just told her go. "And she was happy?"

Shane nodded. "Never saw anyone so happy," he confirmed.

Another question rose to Cris's lips, but she refrained from asking it. Refrained because if she was wrong in what she was thinking, she would feel like a complete idiot. Besides, she was barely holding herself together as it was.

Again, she looked toward the azalea for some kind of guidance. If she didn't know better, she would say that the bush had sprouted even more blossoms since a couple of minutes ago.

Was that even possible?

You're just seeing what you want to see. It's not a magic bush.

"You're a good person, Shane McCallister," she said with affection. She placed her hand on Shane's shoulder, making physical as well as verbal contact.

"That's because I was an Eagle Scout." He added in a deadpan tone, "Remind me to show you my badges some day."

He was kidding, but the statement sparked something serious in her mind. "I was considering enrolling Ricky in the Cub Scouts. Maybe you can give him a few pointers when the time comes."

"Would love to give him pointers," he said, and paused. Finally, unable to take the suspense any longer, he asked, "So? Have you had time to think about it? Would you like to have your name associated with that of a deadly dull general contractor?"

The way he phrased it had her laughing. "You certainly don't know much about salesmanship, do you?"

"If you mean would I give up honesty to sell someone on something, then no, I wouldn't, so I guess that in turn means I don't know the first thing about decent salesmanship," he conceded.

"Trust me. What you lack in salesmanship, you more than make up for with heart. And kindness. Lancelot wasn't considered a dull man—but beneath his fancy coat of mail he was a pretty ordinary guy. Nevertheless, he got to ride to the rescue a lot. Like you."

"Except that I don't actually 'ride to the rescue' a lot," he corrected. His eyes held hers as he said, "Just this once."

"If you do this right, once is more than enough," she told him, her voice dropping to a whisper. Her heart was racing. She was considering doing this, she was actually considering it, she thought.

What "considering"? She *was* going to accept Shane's offer.

"Just so we're clear," Shane asked, because heaven knew, he wasn't at all clear at this point, "is that a yes?"

She nodded very slowly as she told him, "Yes. It's definitely a yes." She put her arms around his neck and rose up on her toes. "Yes," she whispered again for good measure, more strongly this time.

When he brought his lips down to hers, sealing the bargain, Cris could have sworn she heard more blossoms—if it was at all possible—push their way out to cover the azalea bush.

CHAPTER NINETEEN

SHANE REALIZED, AS he drew his head back, that he had gotten caught up in the moment and slipped. And while, judging by Cris's response, she had enjoyed the brief kiss, he knew it shouldn't have happened. It didn't exactly go very far in building her confidence that he intended to keep things between them platonic.

Under no circumstances did he want her to entertain the concern, even for a second, that he might force himself on her. That *wasn't* why he had offered to marry her.

So, pulling himself together, Shane said, "I want you to know that just because I kissed you now, you have nothing to worry about from me. That kiss was simply to seal our bargain," he explained, a gentle smile playing on his lips. "Even though I'll have to move into the inn, it's strictly for appearances. The MacDonalds' investigator would think it odd if we maintained separate home addresses."

"I agree," Cris said, even though a part of her couldn't believe she was having this conversation. It felt like something out of a Jane Austen book, or at the very least, a book written in or about that era. A marriage-of-convenience book that chronicled decorum, not strong emotions such as love or passion. "For appearances," she echoed. "How long do you think—?"

She left the rest unspoken, not quite knowing how to frame the question without sounding as though she didn't want to be tied to him. She didn't want to insult him or hurt his feelings.

Shane filled in the rest of her question, instinctively knowing what she was trying to ask. He honestly couldn't give her a number because he didn't know.

"As long as it takes, I guess. Until the MacDonalds back off and decide it's not worth their time and effort to pursue the matter."

She had a feeling that Marion would continue looking for a way to take Ricky from her out of sheer spite. "In other words, until Ricky's eighteen."

"I wasn't figuring it would go on *that* long, but technically, it could." He looked at Cris for a long moment, thinking that if what he'd just said came to pass, he'd wind up taking a *lot* of cold showers. "Are you prepared for that eventuality?"

"It wasn't me I was worried about." And it wasn't. She was concerned about him. This was a potentially long "jail sentence" for him. "Are you? You're pretty much putting your life on hold indefinitely by doing this."

"So are you," Shane pointed out.

That wasn't quite true. "Ricky *is* my life. Any time that might be left over goes toward my family and keeping the inn in business." Another reason she wouldn't have allowed her father to risk a second mortgage on the inn to cover her legal costs, she thought. Losing to the MacDonalds would be disastrous for the inn as well as the family. "But you—what if tomorrow, or next week, the woman of your dreams crossed your path? You wouldn't be free to do anything about it. Wouldn't be free to explore your options because, as far as the public is concerned, you're already married to me."

He congratulated himself on keeping his feelings for her sufficiently buried so that she hadn't made the connection. With any luck, she never would and he would just be remembered as "the friend" who came through for her.

"The chances of that woman popping up out of the blue are pretty astronomical," he scoffed.

Stranger things had been known to happen. "But say she did, then what?" Cris pressed.

"I'll handle it if the matter comes up," he promised her, dismissing the subject. "Right now, the immediate problem is to secure Ricky's mailing address—and to make sure it's the same as yours."

Cris took a deep breath, still trying to steady her nerves. She was lucky Shane was being so willingly helpful, she thought.

"You're right, of course."

He laughed. "That might carry more weight if you didn't sound as though you were psyching yourself up for something you viewed as challenging—and not in a good way."

She didn't want Shane thinking she was being ungrateful. "Just prewedding jitters. I had them last time, too," she quickly confided. A small smile played on her lips. "This is a lot like that time," she added.

The remark aroused his curiosity and Shane asked, "In what way?"

"I eloped then, too," she told him. "Same reason, in a way," Cris realized.

From what Shane knew, Cris and Mike had run off together because they loved each other. He didn't see the connection. "How's that?"

"It was because of the MacDonalds then, too," Cris explained. "Mike didn't want to have to deal with his parents." Her mouth set in a hard line as the memory returned. "Although they hardly ever paid any attention to him, they made it clear they felt his actions reflected on them."

Shane shook his head. "I'm afraid I still don't see—"

Cris raised her chin, struggling to bank the wave of bitterness she felt. "Marriage to someone like me was completely beneath him."

"In what world?" Shane wanted to know, indignation echoing in his voice.

"Theirs," she replied with a careless shrug.

She pursed her lips. Shane was right. Marrying him was the best way to deal with the threat of Mike's parents. Shane provided Ricky with a "father," who anyone could see, even under scrutiny, was a good, decent, hardworking man. Provided Ricky with a loving, *complete* home. And her having a good lawyer, thanks to Wyatt's connections, should for sure give her nothing to worry about.

Her eyes met Shane's as she allowed him one more chance to bail out. "Are you sure you want to do this?" she asked.

Yes, I want to do this. Because you need me to do this. Because, maybe just for a little while, you actually need me.

Shane looked at her seriously. "Would you feel better if I signed a document to that effect and had it notarized?"

He succeeded in making her laugh, albeit self-consciously. "I guess I do sound a little neurotic," she admitted.

He augmented her admission. "You sound like a concerned mother who is a very good, very fair person. Who also happens to be just a tiny bit neurotic," he added after a brief pause. Then, growing serious, he made a suggestion. "We can leave tonight. The sooner we do this," he continued, "the sooner you'll feel more confident about the situation."

He was right. Again.

Initially, he'd thought they'd fly, but the realities of air travel these days made driving a better option, so he proposed that, instead. "This way we don't have to waste time with airline check-ins and all that hassle. Time-wise, it will probably wind up being the same—except that driving gives us more in control of the situation."

"Yes, but aren't you too tired to drive?"

"Just getting my second wind," he told her. "You can sleep while I'm driving, then we'll switch off and you can take over for the second half of the trip. How's that?" he asked, even though, unless he felt suddenly too tired to keep his eyes open, he intended to drive all the way and just let her sleep. She could probably use the shut-eye after the emotional wringer she'd just been put through.

Cris nodded as she started to go back inside the inn. But a second before she crossed the threshold, she stopped and looked at him. "We're really doing this?"

"Unless you change your mind, we're really doing this," he confirmed without a trace of hesitation.

Flashing a grateful smile at him, Cris brushed her lips against his cheek. "Thank you," she whispered.

"Any time you need to get married, I'm your man," he quipped.

It was a joke, meant to lighten the mood, but deep down, she had a feeling he meant it.

She didn't laugh.

THEY WERE ON the road within the hour, a change of clothes for each of them—something a little more formal and a little less comfortable than what they were currently wearing—packed in a small suitcase that lay on the backseat.

Most of the hour had been spent making arrangements with her family and assuring them that she wasn't just running off to spare them what could very well be an ugly legal confrontation with the MacDonalds.

She convinced her father and sisters when she pointed out that if she was really running off, she would be taking her son with her, not leaving Ricky behind with them.

That finally won over her family.

THE END OF that hour found Richard walking Shane and her to Shane's car.

Thinking that the man might want a few moments alone with his daughter before she set out for Vegas, Shane offered to step out of earshot. But Richard told him that wasn't necessary.

Shane still insisted on giving them their privacy and moved out of hearing range.

Richard took his daughter's hands in his. "I always thought that when you got married again, I'd be there for the ceremony."

Things never did work out just the way they were supposed to, she mused. "Next time," Cris promised with a laugh. "Besides, you know this one is just for appearances, Dad."

Richard nodded, glancing in Shane's direction. "You could do worse, you realize. He's a fine, unselfish young man."

Because there were definite feelings for Shane evolving within her, she deliberately *avoided* looking at him. Instead, she kept her eyes on her father's face. "I know, Dad," she admitted. "But he's doing this because I need help. I wouldn't take advantage of a man who was merely trying to help."

"Maybe he wouldn't mind being taken advantage of," Richard suggested.

"Dad—" The tone was meant to warn her father away from following that line of thinking.

Richard shrugged his thin shoulders, not quite willing to completely give up the subject of Shane being an *actual* husband for Cris.

"I'm just saying…" he told her, letting the rest of his sentence fade away.

Coming forward, Shane made sure to clear his throat so that he had the attention of both of them—and no secrets floated around. "We'd better get going," Shane urged her.

She kissed her father quickly, said, "Tell Ricky when he wakes up tomorrow that

I love him and that I'll be back before he knows it. Don't say anything about the wedding to him," she said. "I want to be the one to tell him about it."

"What'll you say?" Shane asked her as they got into the truck.

She was honest with him. Buckling up, she said, "I haven't got a clue."

Explaining it to Ricky wouldn't be easy—especially since she would have to fabricate a story.

"He'll see through lies," Shane warned. The boy had truly impressed him. At five, Ricky had a better grasp on some things than children a lot older than him. "He's a smart young man."

"He's not *that* smart," she countered. "This is a lot to take in."

Especially, she added silently, if she told him everything. How she and Shane were only pretending to be husband and wife—for his sake.

"The simplest thing," Shane was saying to her, "is to just tell him we got married and I'm going to be his other dad."

"I don't want to lie to him," she protested.

"You're not lying," he pointed out. "The

next time we see him, we will have gotten married. That's the whole purpose of this road trip, remember?"

"Before, you said something about telling Ricky you were his 'other' dad," she said, getting back to a question she had. "Did you actually mean to say that?"

They hit the Santa Ana Freeway. It was surprisingly empty this evening. For the time being, he turned the headlights on high beams.

"No matter what you decide to tell him, I don't want Ricky thinking that I'm going to try to take his dad's place. That might make him balk—and that's the last thing you need.

"Even if we were getting married with the intention of truly beginning a new life together," Shane continued, "I wouldn't want him to think I was replacing his dad. Just being another dad to him would be enough."

It was a beautiful sentiment and hearing him say that warmed her heart. She admired his thoughtfulness and the way he could put himself into someone else's shoes—small shoes in this case—and understand how someone thought. That was rare in a person, she couldn't help noting.

"You're right," she told Shane.

He smiled in response. "I am," he agreed, then expanded on the subject just to tease her a little. "Not every time, granted, but a lot."

Cris laughed, getting a kick out of Shane even under all the pressure. "Now *that* sounds like a husband."

"I guess we've got our roles down pat," he said with a grin.

Were they just roles, she wanted to ask, or were they something more? Dress rehearsal for the real thing?

But instead of pressing home the point, she let the subject go.

It was easier that way.

LESS THAN EIGHTEEN hours after they had taken off for Las Vegas, they were back in Shane's truck, returning to San Diego and the Ladera-by-the-Sea Inn.

It was a bright, sunny day and Cris watched in fascination at the way the sunlight shone on the ring on her finger.

The *new* ring.

Currently, the surface of her ring was turning a sunbeam into an explosion of warm rainbow colors that bounced around the interior of the vehicle.

"You really are an Eagle Scout," she said. "Most men wouldn't actually bring a wedding ring to their spur-of-the-moment wedding." She looked up from the ring, something belatedly occurring to her. "This was your wife's, wasn't it?"

He didn't want her taking it off, claiming some superstition or other. The ring looked right on her hand, like it belonged there. "She would have approved of my marrying you to keep your former in-laws from getting their clutches on Ricky. She was always rooting for the good guy to win—or in your case, the good girl."

"Your late wife must have been a really nice person." That sounded so trite to her ear, she decided. But she really did mean the sentiment, she thought, frustrated.

"She was," Shane assured her. "And I have a feeling she would have liked you," he added.

She supposed that it was silly, but hearing Shane tell her that made her feel warm inside. As if, just for a couple of hours, she was actually immersed in the world they were verbally creating as they went along.

She turned the ring on her finger, still amazed that it was there. She'd worn Mike's ring until this morning, and although the rings were astonishingly the same size and similar in appearance, it still felt different on her finger.

Cris wondered if it was just her mind playing tricks on her.

She shifted in her seat and, though restrained by the seat belt, she managed to turn her body toward Shane. "I can't believe how fast you can get married in Vegas. It was even faster than when Mike and I got married at city hall."

He wasn't about to dispute the impression. "They like to pride themselves on how effortlessly you can get married there. No hoops to jump through, no waiting period, just one-two-three and you're husband and wife." He also had a corollary to the heavy volume of quickie marriages. "Don't forget they also deal heavily in painless divorces."

She thought about that for a minute, then laughed. "I guess Vegas is the only place you can get married, divorced, win a fortune and then lose it all in less than a week's time. I wonder what the record for that is."

"Most likely you can find the information somewhere on the internet. Except for advertising my work online, I don't have that much occasion to use it," he confided. They'd been driving awhile now. He took his eyes off the desolate road for a second and slanted a glance in her direction. "Do you want to stop somewhere to eat, or do you want to drive straight through and just get home?"

"I don't know about you," she said, "but that lunch we had after we left that funny little chapel certainly filled me up."

"Yeah, me, too. Okay, we'll drive straight through," he told her. "Have you figured out yet what you're going to tell Ricky?"

She had, and she had Shane to thank for that. He was turning out to be a very handy man to have around, she thought fondly.

"I think what you suggested earlier is the best approach. Smart or not, I don't want to overload Ricky with lengthy explanations. Besides, if this thing does wind up going to Family Court and those horrible people have their lawyer put Ricky on the stand for some reason, I don't want them grilling him until there's some kind of a slipup on his part. I wouldn't put it past those people to use Ricky until they get their own way." She paused for a moment, then said, "In case I didn't say it before, thank you for doing this."

Shane laughed. "Yes, you did say it before, but I don't think you've mentioned it this hour," he teased.

Cris inclined her head. "I guess I am repeating myself, but I *really* can't thank you enough for doing this."

"I believe the proper response to that is— no big deal," Shane told her.

"But it is," she insisted with feeling. "This is a *huge* deal. I can't exactly go to Husbands Are Us and get a loaner father for Ricky. And as a family unit, our chances of beating that woman and her heartless husband increase a hundredfold—even if I can't buy and sell a whole town the way they can.

"If you hadn't ridden to the rescue," she told him, "I just might have given in to my inner coward and right now, Ricky and I would be driving for parts unknown with the future before us reduced to a glaring question mark."

He knew better than that, Shane thought. "No, you wouldn't," he contradicted her.

He said that as if he actually believed it. "What makes you so sure?"

"Because you're a fighter," he told her simply. "You might speak softly and keep things to yourself for the most part, but nobody's going to push you around. One look into those mesmerizing blue eyes of yours and anyone who's paying any attention at all would know that you are a tiger when it comes to fighting for things that are important to you."

He almost had her convinced. Oh, how she'd love to be the person he was verbally painting. "You sound like you think you know me better than I know myself."

His smile was laid-back. "Maybe I do," he said. "I don't just see and hear—I *pay attention*," Shane added. "And like I told you, I'm usually right."

I hope so, Shane. I certainly do hope so, Cris thought as she turned her eyes back on the deserted road taking them home.

CHAPTER TWENTY

RICKY WAS THE first one to see his mother and Shane when they walked into the inn that afternoon.

The little boy had been sitting forlornly on the floor in the main room, listlessly watching the door. He would become tense, according to what Alex later told her, each time it opened, only to slump in disappointment when whoever entered was not her.

The moment he saw her and Shane, Ricky lit up almost as brightly as the tree he was next to. He jumped to his feet, shot across the floor and had his arms wrapped around Cris's hips before she had a chance to take more than one step into the inn.

"Mama, you're back!" Ricky cried excitedly, beaming so hard she thought it would hurt his face. "You didn't leave me!"

Stooping, Cris gathered the boy into her arms and picked him up. "Boy, you've gained weight since I've been gone," she teased. "All muscle, I bet."

"Uh-huh." He nodded vigorously.

"And you *know* I would never leave you," she said, growing more serious. "I just had to take a quick little trip, that's all."

"With Shane?" Ricky asked, peering around her shoulder at the man standing beside her.

"With Shane," Cris confirmed. "He was a very important part of the little trip."

"And I couldn't come?" Ricky queried. In his whole lifetime, he and his mother had *never* been separated for longer than his kindergarten sessions.

"Not this time, Ricky," she told him.

"But next time?" He looked at her hopefully, his bright blue eyes pleading for an affirmative answer.

There wouldn't be a "next time," not like this one. But no point in getting into that now. It would only confuse her son.

"Next time," she assured him just to lay the matter to rest.

"I tried to tell him you were coming back and he could go to his room," Alex said, running her hand over Ricky's head, "but he wouldn't budge. Insisted on staying right here by the tree and waiting for you," she said.

"So…?" Richard asked, looking from Cris to Shane. The rest of his question hung unspoken in the air. But then, everyone knew what he was asking about, with the exception of Ricky, who still clung to her, afraid to release her because she might leave again.

Shifting Ricky onto her hip the way she used to carry him when he was smaller, Cris held up her left hand. The diamond-accented band did the talking for her.

Richard smiled, nodding. He moved over to Shane, took the younger man's hand and pumped it heartily while clapping him on the back. "Welcome to the family, boy."

Ricky looked from his grandfather to Shane and finally at his mother. "Why is Grandpa welcoming Shane to the family? Did you adopt him?" he wanted to know.

Cris laughed despite herself and shook her head. "No. Ricky, Shane and I got married."

She approached the subject gingerly, not knowing what to expect once she told the boy what she felt was safe to tell him. She knew he liked Shane, but he liked him as a friend, not as his father. She wasn't sure how he would react to the news she'd just given him and held her breath for a moment, waiting.

"Why?" Ricky asked, his eyebrows wrinkling in his confusion.

"So I could take care of you and be around when you or your mom needs someone," Shane explained, cutting in and answering before Cris had the chance.

Ricky fell silent for a long moment and Cris was worried that her son was taking the news the wrong way, viewing Shane as an invader.

So she was very surprised, not to mention immensely relieved, when her son suddenly smiled and said, "Cool. Does that mean you'll be my dad now?" he inquired, looking up at Shane.

Cris almost felt giddy. She'd worried for no reason at all. With a sigh of relief, she set Ricky down on the floor. "Are you okay with that?"

"Sure!" She'd put herself through torture for no reason, apparently. Ricky, meanwhile, had presented himself to his new dad and asked, "Wanna play catch with me and Wyatt?"

"Oh, so *now* you want to play catch," Wyatt spoke up, pretending to be offended. "After I couldn't get you to leave this room."

"I'd love to, Ricky," Shane told the boy, "but I really should get back to work." He slanted a glance at his new father-in-law in name only.

Richard waved his hand. "The work'll wait. Go play catch with Ricky," he urged.

Shane inclined his head in acknowledgment. "You're the boss," he told the older man.

"Actually, that would be Cris's title," Richard said with a laugh. "But I'll fill in for the time being."

Excited, Ricky grabbed Wyatt's hand with one of his and Shane's hand with the other. Wyatt looked over his shoulder toward Alex. "Fill Cris in for me," he told her.

"Fill me in on what?" Cris asked, forcing herself to tear her eyes away from the sight of Ricky "bonding" with his new father. As much as it warmed her heart to see this, she couldn't help worrying how Ricky would react when he found out that it was all just a charade, undertaken so that he could continue living with her. Would her son then be grateful for her efforts, or angry because he'd been lied to?

Nothing was simple anymore, she thought, fighting despair. But now wasn't the time to brood.

She faced her older sister and asked, "What's going on, Alex?"

"Don't look as if you expect me to pull a ghost out of my pocket. What I have to tell you is a good thing," Alex prefaced, then got straight to the bottom line and told Cris what she needed to be aware of. "Wyatt called that lawyer friend of his last night—"

"I know that." He'd been on the phone when she'd run out of the inn, overwhelmed.

"What you don't know is that the lawyer dropped everything and hopped on a commuter plane this morning. He was here for a little while, talking to us, and Wyatt's right. This guy is fantastic."

Cris wasn't ready to cheer just yet. She needed details. "Define fantastic," Cris said.

"He got right on your case the second he hung up with Wyatt yesterday. The investigator his firm employs immediately started digging into your past and Shane's past."

And this was a good thing? Cris thought. What was she missing?

"Hold it," she exclaimed. "The investigator dug into *our* pasts? If anything, I would have thought that he'd dig into the MacDonalds' past."

"Travis—that's Wyatt's lawyer friend," Stevi said, eagerly picking up the thread of the story, her eyes shining, "wanted to find out what he'd be up against. You *know* that those people would have you investigated with a high-power magnifying glass. Travis just wanted to see if they'd find anything."

"And?" Cris asked.

She knew there was absolutely nothing compromising in her past, but she wasn't really knowledgeable about Shane's. She assumed there would be nothing bad, but she would have been the first to admit she was naive when it came to the ways of the world.

Cris held her breath as she waited for either Alex or Stevi to fill her in.

"And so far, you and Shane are in first place for the Mr. and Mrs. Norman Rockwell award," Stevi told her with a huge grin, falling back on her art history knowledge to cite the popular late artist whose drawings became synonymous with family values and normalcy.

"He couldn't uncover so much as a single blemish in either of you," Alex told her.

"Which I find a very comforting thing," Richard said, speaking up. And then he grinned. "It's not every father who gets to have an extensive background check run on a son-in-law."

"Fake son-in-law," Cris reminded him. "Shane's just doing me a tremendous favor."

Stevi appeared skeptical. "You two didn't stop for a quickie honeymoon before coming home?" she asked.

Cris shot her younger sister a quelling look. "That wasn't part of the arrangement," she reminded Stevi.

The skepticism gave way to disappointment. "Too bad," she said with a deep sigh.

Cris pretended to just ignore Stevi and drop the subject, but inside, she could feel something echoing Stevi's very sentiment. Granted she and Shane were just pretending for the benefit of the MacDonalds and their lawyer—but they *were* legally married and…

And nothing, she upbraided herself.

"If you'll excuse me, I'd better get to my kitchen." She knew Jorge would have pitched in and taken her place, but the meals at the inn were her responsibility. "I've got some catching up to do," she told the others.

Nodding, Alex imparted one final piece of information. "Travis said he'd get back to us when he had anything to share."

Cris paused to acknowledge that she'd heard her sister, praying at the same time that the call would come soon. She couldn't really breathe a sigh of relief until she was certain the MacDonalds' threat was null and void.

"You sure you want me to put my things in here?" Shane asked that evening, still holding the suitcase he'd hastily thrown together for their impromptu trip yesterday. To add substance to their charade, he'd moved into the inn as she'd proposed. But he hadn't thought he'd be moving into her room. "I don't require much space—I could sack out in your Dad's office. Nobody would be the wiser," he added. His point was that she could keep her privacy while they pretended to live together.

"I'm sure," Cris said, answering his question. "I don't want to risk the MacDonalds' investigator finding out that we've got separate sleeping arrangements. I just *know* they'd use that to say I was unbalanced or had some sort of emotional issues. Since we're doing this, humor me. I don't want to take any unnecessary chances with these people."

He couldn't argue with that. "Understood." Shane glanced around the small suite Richard had given Cris after she'd married Mike. Tastefully furnished to make a person feel at home, it had a queen-size bed on one side and a writing table and love seat on the other. "I'll take the couch," he told her.

"It's a love seat," she corrected.

He shrugged, setting down his suitcase. "Same difference."

"Actually, it isn't," she explained. "A love seat is smaller." She regarded his height. He was at least six feet tall if not taller. "Probably too small to accommodate you."

Unfazed, he laughed. "That's okay, I fold

up." He grinned at her. "Don't look so concerned," he added. "I can sleep standing up if I have to. The love seat'll be fine."

Another man would have complained about the inconvenience. That he didn't was just another testament to his strength of character.

"You are incredibly flexible," she marveled.

Her choice of words made him smile. "Comes in handy," he responded, nodding at the love seat. Shane left his suitcase on the floor beside it. "Okay, I've got to get back to work or your father will think that I've let pretending to be his son-in-law go to my head and made me a slacker."

"Not that my father would *ever* think that, but if he did, I'd defend you," she told him, responding in kind to his playful tone. "Hopefully," she added, a bit more subdued, "you won't have to suffer like this too long."

Shane had a feeling, as he left the room, that Cris and he had entirely different definitions of the word "suffer."

FOR THE NEXT two weeks, Cris felt she was living each hour of each day in painful limbo.

Waiting to have this situation with her son resolved was absolutely killing her.

She had communicated with Wyatt's lawyer a number of times and found the man's soft-spoken self-confidence immensely reassuring. To his credit, Travis Kelly seemed exceedingly on top of things.

So much so that when he told her not to worry, she almost didn't—the operative word being "almost."

But because Cris knew that legal issues were not straightforward, that the wild card in this lawsuit was ultimately the judge she would draw, she did continue to worry. Judges could overrule decisions, go in whatever direction they felt was right—or for that matter, any direction they wanted to go in, citing technicalities.

All judges, she was well aware, were not created equal, and if she drew one swayed by wealth or impressed with the MacDonalds and their standing in society, she was doomed. Married or not, she was the daughter of an innkeeper and family funds were limited, whereas the MacDonalds could have bought and sold her a hundred times over.

Some people would be impressed with that. Even judges.

"Everything will be all right," Shane told her as he walked into her work area in the kitchen. It was lunchtime and the first wave of guests had come and gone, while the second wave had not gotten started yet.

She was startled when she heard Shane's voice. "I didn't hear you come in."

"That's because you're worrying too hard. Don't," he told her, feathering his fingertips along her forehead, smoothing out the worry lines. "You're not going to lose custody of Ricky."

Her heart was pounding, and she knew that it had little to do with anxiety at the moment. But she focused on what he said and not on what he'd just caused to happen with his gentle touch.

"You can't know that," she insisted.

Shane wasn't about to argue with her—but he wasn't about to back down, either. "Let's just say it's a gut feeling."

She fervently wished she could believe him. "What's your gut's track record?"

He pretended to think. "Nine-eight—no, ninety-nine-point-one."

"Impressive," she conceded, although she knew he was pulling her leg to get her to lighten up.

Shane grew serious. Despite Jorge's presence in the room, he refrained from lowering his voice as he made a vow. "I won't let the MacDonalds take Ricky away from you. That's a promise."

Cris forced a smile to her lips, knowing he was the one inconvenienced by all this, the one who had sacrificed normalcy to help her. She couldn't expect more from him— yet he kept giving more. "What will you do, challenge Mike's parents to a joust?"

That wasn't what he'd meant, but since she'd mentioned it, he pretended to consider a duel on horseback. "That's an idea. I know I could take MacDonald," he told her.

If such a confrontation were possible, she had no doubts that Shane would win within the first three minutes. "Especially since Arthur probably can't even sit on a horse."

"Arthur?" He pretended to look surprised that she would pit him against her former father-in-law. "I was thinking along the lines of fighting the tough one—Marion."

Cris laughed then, feeling infinitely better. He kept doing that for her, lightening her mood no matter how dark her thoughts became. Cris was immensely grateful to him for that.

Gazing at him with appreciation, she said, "Thank you."

Her words of gratitude had come out of nowhere. "For?" he asked.

"For making something unbearable bearable." She couldn't put it any better than that, despite knowing in all honesty that there was more to what she was feeling than simply gratitude. With his kindnesses mounting and his efforts to keep her courage up and her faith intact, she was beginning to feel that she was falling in love with Shane.

Shane wasn't about to take undue credit, especially since he was only doing the only decent thing. "You've got your family's support."

"True, but having you pretend to be my husband, that's the part that's going to make a judge decide in my favor." She looked at him, eyes shining with thankfulness.

"I'm happy to help," he told her.

She was about to say something more to him on the subject, when Stevi burst into the kitchen. She appeared surprised and then pleased to find Shane there.

"Oh, good, you're here, too," Stevi said. "This makes it easier."

"Makes *what* easier? What's up?" Cris asked, becoming immobile with fear.

"Travis is here," Stevi told them, then looked at her sister. "The lawyer Wyatt got for you."

"I know who Travis is, Stevi," she snapped, then gazed at her sister, chagrinned. "Sorry."

"Apology accepted," Stevi said, brushing Cris's words aside.

Cris was already wiping her hands on a kitchen towel. After tossing it on the work-table, she tried to untie her apron strings. She was so nervous she wound up pulling them into a knot instead.

"Here, let me," Shane said, getting behind her. With a few swift movements, he untied the knot, setting her and the apron free.

"Did he say what he was doing here?" Cris asked. So far, all her communication with the lawyer had been restricted to the tele-phone.

Stevi shook her head. "All he said was

he had some news and wanted to tell you in person."

Hearing that, Cris felt as if her knees had suddenly evaporated. She could barely breathe. "Oh, Lord, did he say how bad it was?"

Stevi looked a little confused by the question. "He didn't say it was bad."

"They come in person when it's bad," Cris said, fear making her sound stilted. She crossed the floor quickly to the swinging kitchen door. "They always come in person."

"Who always comes in person?" Shane asked her, trying hard to understand what she was referring to.

Her eyes appeared haunted as she turned to him. "When they have bad news to tell you, they come in person to soften the blow."

He realized then that she was referring to the chaplain and the marine officer who had come to tell her that her husband had been killed. Cris was reliving the trauma.

Shane took her hand in his and squeezed it, silently giving her his support. "You don't know that for a fact. He's a lawyer. Lawyers are a breed unto themselves. They do things according to their own rules." He turned to Stevi. "Where is he, Stevi?"

"He's waiting for you in Dad's office," Stevi answered.

Shane nodded. "Okay, let's go," he said to Cris.

"You don't have to come," she said, the words barely exiting her exceedingly dry mouth. This was her fight, not his.

"Yeah, I do," he told her firmly. "Whatever it is, I'm in this with you for the long haul. End of discussion."

His words won her undying gratitude. At that moment—and forever.

CHAPTER TWENTY-ONE

TRAVIS ROSE FROM the desk he'd temporarily commandeered as Cris and Shane, along with Stevi, entered the room.

"I came as soon as I had a chance to check my source and verify the information." Travis looked from Cris to Shane, scrutinizing their expressions and demeanors. Cris looked as if she was holding her breath, waiting for ghosts to come popping out of the shadows. It told him what he needed to know. "I take it that the two of you haven't heard yet."

"Heard what?" Shane asked the lawyer as they all sat down, Stevi in a chair off to the side, he and Cris facing Travis.

Shane didn't know whether to brace himself for Cris's sake. According to Wyatt, Travis Kelly was a high-powered attorney with a great track record, but it was difficult to picture him that way. For one thing, Travis looked too young to be a high-powered anything. What he *did* look like was someone who played backup guitar in a band, or maybe even the drummer.

But brilliant lawyer? Not even the navy designer suit he had on delivered a convincing argument in favor of that.

Still, Cris seemed happy with the way Travis was handling the case, and in the end, hers was the only opinion that mattered, he reminded himself. He had to remember not to take his role as her "husband" so seriously.

Rather than answer Shane's question directly, Travis told them, smiling widely, "You won't have to worry about Marion and Arthur MacDonald being a threat any longer."

"You killed them?" Stevi asked. All eyes turned toward her.

Since she'd been the one to relay that the lawyer wanted to talk to them, she'd felt entitled to sit in on the meeting and find out firsthand what was going on. That she was also more than just a little attracted to this friend of Wyatt's had only increased her desire to remain in the room.

Amused at her out-of-left-field guess, Travis laughed. "Even if I had, Stevi, I couldn't exactly admit to that, now could I?"

"No court in the world would have convicted you," Stevi said with a little more verve than was called for. "Especially not if—"

"Stevi!" Cris said sharply, reining her sister in before the younger woman got too carried away. "What's happened?" she asked Travis, turning back to him. "*Why* aren't Ricky's grandparents a threat any longer?"

"Because currently," Travis replied, "they have a bigger battle on their hands than taking custody of Ricky from you."

"What kind of a battle?" Cris wanted to know.

Granted, he was drawing this out, Travis thought, but he decided Travis could be forgiven since the matter would have such a good finish. "Staying out of jail."

Clearly bewildered, Cris shook her head. "I don't understand," she told the lawyer.

Travis slid forward in the padded office chair, creating an air of shared confidence. "Although undoubtedly a great deal more has yet to come to light, the important points have already been made. The law frowns on insider trading and your former in-laws are guilty of just that—big-time," he underscored.

Cris knew that was illegal, but wasn't it one of those slap-on-the-wrist-don't-do-it-again crimes? If so, it didn't really help her in the long run. "But even if they get convicted, they won't be put in jail forever, will they?"

"No," Travis agreed. "Not forever. Just long enough to establish the kind of people they are. Trust me, no family court judge will take custody away from a married mother with a spotless reputation and hand over a child to two ex-convicts, no matter *how* rich they are," he promised.

It sounded almost too good to be true. She was afraid to let her guard down, afraid to allow hope to take over, because the disappointment would just be too devastating if things worked out otherwise.

So she had to ask. "It's really over?" The question came out hesitantly, as if actually uttering the words would somehow jinx the whole thing and turn it sour.

"It's really over," Travis assured her in a kind, understanding voice.

Tears sprang to her eyes as she breathed a huge sigh of relief and cried, "Oh, thank you!"

Travis laughed softly. "Much as I'd like to take the credit for this and say it was due to my sharp, legal mind coupled with having the cunning of a fox, in all honesty I'm only the messenger in this case. I didn't twist the MacDonalds' arms into participating in insider trading—which was most likely not just a one-time event.

"I might have, of course," he continued, an enigmatic smile playing on his lips, "encouraged my investigator to share an after-hours drink or two with his close friend who just happened to be a well-known reporter with a prominent newspaper." Which was why the story was spreading as quickly as it was, condemning the MacDonalds in the court of public opinion. "If you really want to thank someone," he told Cris, "thank the MacDonalds."

"How do you figure that?" Shane asked him.

The expression on the lawyer's face said

the question was simple enough to answer. "Well, if they didn't have the colossal egos that they do, thinking themselves not just above the law, but too clever to be caught or even challenged, we might not have cause to celebrate right now."

He rose from behind her father's desk and paused to shake each of their hands. "Congratulations," he told Cris. "It's a bouncing five-year-old."

It was beginning to sink in. She wouldn't have to worry. Ricky was safe. "I can't thank you enough," Cris said with genuine appreciation.

"Just enjoy your little boy. That's thanks enough," the lawyer told her. Turning toward Stevi, Travis nodded. "Tell Wyatt I'll see him at the wedding."

Stevi's eyes lit up. "You're coming to the wedding?"

"Wouldn't miss it for the world," Travis said with sincerity. He took his leave after saying one final thing. "Feel free to call me if you have any further questions, but if I were you, I'd consider this whole matter put to bed—once and for all."

Shane looked at Cris. "I guess this qualifies as a Christmas miracle."

She wiped away the tears that just refused to stop falling. The release was tremendous. "Works for me," she told him.

"Okay if I tell Dad and the others, or do you want to be the one?" Stevi asked her.

Cris knew Stevi was dying to spread the word. "Go right ahead," she said. "I'm just going to stand here for a few more minutes and savor this feeling."

Nodding, Stevi hurried from the room to inform the others that Ricky was safe now, once and for all.

Cris was hardly aware her sister had left the room. She was almost numb with relief. But amid the incredible surge of joy, she acknowledged one tiny downside to the news Travis had delivered.

Shane wouldn't need to keep up the charade any longer.

She looked at him now, searching for the right way to say what was on her mind without sounding petty or ungrateful.

Or greedy.

She supposed that the only way to say it was to say it. She forced a smile to her lips, but she had trouble maintaining it. "I guess this means you're free."

He stared at her, not quite able to follow her thinking. "Free?"

She nodded. Why was she feeling suddenly sad? Ricky was safe, that was all that mattered. Right? "You don't have to pretend to be my husband anymore."

"Technically, I'm not pretending," Shane reminded her. "We did get legally married by a justice of the peace." He drew a breath. Shane didn't particularly like what he was going to say next. "Which means we'll have to get legally divorced."

She nodded numbly as reluctance took hold of her. She didn't *want* to divorce him. But she also knew that, reasonably, she couldn't be selfish and try to postpone the event by dragging her feet—as much as she really wanted to.

What was going on with her? Cris silently demanded. The threat was over. She'd won her case. There was no need to pretend anymore.

"When do you want to do that? Start the process," she added when he looked at her blankly.

Never, Shane thought. He realized that something within him had begun to hope that if they remained married long enough, Cris might get used to the idea and, well, perhaps grow to like it—and him—enough to be his wife not just in name, but in fact.

"Up to you," he replied. There was no emotion in his voice.

She paused, gathering her courage. Maybe it was because of her initial exhilaration that she heard herself saying, "Would you mind very much if we waited until after Christmas and Alex's wedding to file for divorce? It's only for a week longer and there's so much going on right now and I'm so busy." She realized she was talking faster and faster and she forced herself to slow down. The new pace lasted less than half a minute. "But then again, you've been so wonderful about all this that I don't want you to think I'm letting the matter slide or taking advantage of you, even if—"

She gazed at him in surprise as he laid a finger to her lips, stopping her increasingly nervous chatter.

"It's okay," Shane assured her. "If you want to wait and put off filing papers for a while, that's okay." He laughed shortly. "It's not as if I'm in any hurry to get this over with."

She stared at him in wonder. "You're not?"

Judiciously, he told her the harmless part. "To be honest, I kind of like hearing Ricky call me Daddy and I'd miss that."

That was easy enough to deal with. It was the least she could do. "He doesn't have to stop calling you that. I mean…" She glanced down, then raised her eyes to his again. "I forgot about Ricky," she admitted. "I don't mean I forgot about *him,* but I forgot about how setting you free would affect him."

That was the second time she'd used the word "free" in connection with his situation. He really wished she wouldn't.

"I'm not exactly in bondage here, Cris. Setting me 'free' indicates I'm a prisoner in this. I'm not," he told her. "And I certainly don't feel like one."

"You don't?" she asked in a hushed voice, trying to get hold of her feelings, which were becoming jumbled in response to his touch.

"No, I don't," he told her. "Not at all."

She deliberately looked away, afraid what he might see in her if he kept eye contact.

"Being 'married' to me had to be frustrating, though. After all, it put your social life on hold."

"That's not why it was frustrating," Shane told her before he could think to censor his words. "And in case you hadn't noticed, I didn't exactly have a social life before I volunteered to marry you so you could keep custody of Ricky."

"Well, I did sort of notice you didn't rush off to meet someone at the end of the day," she admitted. "But I just thought you were a very hard worker and were trying to finish the renovations on the inn as fast as possible." The rest of his words played themselves back in her head, arousing her curiosity. "Why *was* it frustrating?"

He was busy coming to terms with what had just happened, and her question hit him out of the blue. "Excuse me?"

"You said that putting your social life on hold wasn't why being 'married' to me was frustrating," Cris repeated. "Why *was* it frustrating?"

"Since we had agreed to make this a marriage of convenience, I had to keep all my natural instincts in check," he explained.

"I couldn't let myself touch you like this." He illustrated his point, ever so lightly gliding his fingertips along her face, pushing a strand of hair away from her eyes. "Or hold you like this," he continued, slipping his arms around her waist and drawing her gently to him. "Or kiss you the way I wanted to," he whispered, lowering his face until only inches separated them.

She could feel her heart pounding wildly, could feel all the stirrings she'd felt earlier but magnified tenfold and clustered so that they were exceedingly hard for her to resist.

His eyes held her captive as she told him in a whisper that was barely audible, "I wouldn't have pushed you away if you had done all those things."

Unable to hold back any longer, the next moment he was kissing her.

The moment after that, they were springing apart as if both had suddenly stepped on spring-loaders. They were no longer alone.

Cris's father, her sisters, Wyatt and Ricky had descended on them en masse, their raised, jovial voices blending inharmoniously to heap congratulations on Cris and Shane before they even walked into the room.

She dearly loved her family, Cris thought, but she would really have liked for them to come in at least a couple of minutes later, allowing her to enjoy what had been ended so abruptly.

Even so, although that kiss hadn't run its course, Cris had arrived at the realization that she was in love with this pretend husband of hers. In love with him, and not at all willing to cast asunder what a roly-poly man in an ill-fitting suit had legalized in the gambling capital of the country.

And she had a feeling, Cris thought, glancing at him as her family swarmed around them, shaking hands and kissing, that Shane knew.

What was she going to do about that?

"Didn't I tell you that Travis was good?" Wyatt was asking her, pleased beyond words that things had turned out this way without having Cris and Ricky put through any sort of lengthy ordeal. Since he sincerely cared about both of them, this meant a lot to him.

"You did that," Cris agreed, giving the man she had grown up with and regarded as a brother a huge, grateful hug.

"But even I didn't think it would be over with this fast," Wyatt admitted.

"Now I won't have to feel guilty about going through with the wedding," Alex said, joining her voice with Wyatt's.

"There was nothing to feel guilty about," Cris told her. "Your impending wedding was practically the only thing that kept me going at times," she told the duo.

Stevi suddenly realized that she was still in charge of the event. The prospect of losing Ricky had put everything on hold, but now it was business as usual. Stevi jumped in with both feet.

"We've got less than a week, people, and we've dropped the ball. From now on, we need to focus, focus, focus. Otherwise, this will *not* go off as planned—do I make myself clear?"

"Oh, Lord, she's back," Andy lamented, rolling her eyes.

"No, she isn't," Ricky said, confused. "She never went away."

"Out of the mouths of babes." Alex laughed, shaking her head.

"I'm not a baby," Ricky protested. Sticking his thumb into his chest, he declared,

"I'm a big boy. Right, Daddy?" he asked, seeking backup from the new man in his life.

"Right you are," Shane agreed. "But now I've got to get back to work," he said, directing his words this time to Richard.

"I can help!" Ricky quickly volunteered, falling into step beside him as Shane began to walk out of the room. The little boy was fairly skipping, taking two steps to each one of Shane's.

Shane was about to tell the boy to remain with his mother, but glancing back over his shoulder, he saw that she was waving her son on.

"It's okay, Ricky. Just be sure to listen to everything he tells you—and follow it to the letter. Understand?"

"Understand," Ricky crowed, excited. Tucking his hand into Shane's, he went happily off.

"You know, anyone seeing that would think they really were father and son," Richard commented.

"I know," Cris replied quietly.

Telling Ricky that Shane wouldn't be his daddy anymore was going to be just awful, she thought. She could feel her stomach tying itself into a knot at the mere idea.

But she knew the job was hers. She just needed to get her strength together to do it.

CHAPTER TWENTY-TWO

HE MOVED HIS things out of Cris's bedroom that evening.

There was no longer a need to keep up the appearance of a real marriage. But because Shane was now working close to eighteen hours a day—doing the things that *didn't* involve major disruptions and create jarring noise in the early hours as well as the late ones, and the noisy work only during the day—Richard insisted that he remain in one of the inn's rooms as a guest. Since that allowed him to remain in proximity to Cris, Shane couldn't get himself to turn down the offer.

Shane worked hard and long, as if his sanity depended on it, because in a way it did. Being so busy during the day gave him no time to think.

That, however, proved impossible.

It seemed to him that no matter what he

was doing, whether working on the renovations or creating the new wing, images of Cris would pop up in his mind, unbidden. The way she tilted her chin, the way she laughed at something he'd said or done, making him feel they were sharing a private moment. The way her lips pursed when she was having a dream. All that was branded in his brain.

He knew he couldn't keep running from the truth. He was in love with her.

And all the while, Christmas and Alex and Wyatt's wedding were drawing steadily closer and closer. When the day finally arrived, it would signal the beginning of the end of his make-believe marriage to Cris. She'd said she was postponing filing for divorce until then.

"Then" no longer seemed far away at all.

With each hour that went by, no matter what he was doing, Shane found himself resisting the idea of the end more and more.

The right thing to do, he knew, was to just let it happen. Let Cris go on with her life and he would go on with his.

But he didn't want to do "the right thing." If he just allowed things to unfold the way they seemed destined to unfold, he would wind up never forgiving himself. Because he'd wind up alone.

For better or worse, he had to make his feelings known, had to state his case, however clumsily, to Cris. If, after he said his piece, she still wanted to go through with the divorce, he wouldn't stand in her way, wouldn't try to talk her out of it. He'd accept her decision.

But before any of that transpired, first he wanted her to hear his side of it.

The question was when?

Because Cris seemed as busy as he was, he really didn't want to ruin what little free time she did have by putting her on the spot. So he let one day slip by, then two, then three. One day fed into another, and before he knew it, it was Christmas Eve, a time, he'd discovered earlier, that Cris and her family celebrated the holiday with their traditional Christmas Eve dinner and then exchanged their gifts.

Since it was a family celebration, Shane was completely surprised when Richard came up to him and asked him to attend.

"If you don't have any other plans," the older man qualified.

It took Shane a moment to replay the man's words in his head and convince himself that his ears weren't playing tricks on him.

"No, I don't have any other plans," he replied. Realizing that he must have sounded monotone and stilted, he explained, "I guess I'm just surprised that you'd invite me."

"Well, you're still officially Cris's husband, so of course you're invited," Richard said, as if there was no other way to regard the current situation between his daughter and Shane. "Eight o'clock all right with you?" Richard asked, then added, "That's when we always have Christmas Eve dinner."

"Eight o'clock's great," Shane said with enthusiasm. "I'll be there."

"Oh," Richard doubled back to tell him one final thing. "As you know we exchange gifts after dinner, but please don't feel obligated to bring anything. You've already done so much," Richard assured him before he went back to his office to tend to some last-minute matters.

"Not nearly as much as I'd like to do," Shane said under his breath.

EVERYONE IN THE Roman family, as well as Wyatt, made him feel at home.

They no longer had a reason to go out of their way and pretend he was part of the family and yet, Shane thought as he sat at the table, finishing his meal and taking part in the conversation, that was exactly the way Cris's family was behaving.

As if he were one of them.

Shane did his best to absorb as much of the event as he could. He was well aware that this might be the next-to-last time he'd be sitting here like this, with Cris on one side of him and Ricky on the other.

If things didn't wind up going the way he hoped tonight, he'd have no choice but to file for that divorce.

The very thought of it pinched his stomach.

"*Now* can I unwrap my presents?" Ricky asked his mother in a barely patient voice as he pushed away his empty plate.

"What makes you think you have any

presents to unwrap?" Wyatt deadpanned. "Maybe Santa's running late tonight."

"I got at least one present," Ricky told him. "I saw Daddy putting a big box under the tree."

"Maybe that was for me," Richard suggested, joining in teasing his grandson.

But Ricky wasn't about to be swayed. "Nah, it's got my name on it. I checked," he said as if he were more young man than little boy.

"Nothing gets by you, does it?" Shane laughed with affection, giving the boy a hug.

Ricky endured the hug for a moment before wriggling out of it. "So can I?" he wanted to know, rocking in his seat. "Can I go open my presents?"

"Tell you what, why don't we all go to the main room to open our presents?" Alex suggested.

"The dishes won't magically do themselves," Cris pointed out as she began to stack them.

Richard put his hand over his daughter's to still them. "Maybe they will, just this once," he told her with a wink.

He coaxed her toward the main room,

knowing the dishes would be taken care of by Jorge, who'd volunteered to do cleanup so they could enjoy the rest of their evening.

Richard, as the patriarch, was in charge of the gift distribution. As always, there was something for everyone. Richard always made sure of that.

Shane's gift to Ricky turned out to be a miniature tool belt with tools that looked like the real deal, but were designed for use by a boy his age.

"Now I can *really* help you," the boy crowed gleefully.

"You might live to regret giving him that," Cris predicted with a laugh. She was enjoying Ricky's reaction to everything. It pleased her that despite the way they all doted on him, Ricky never behaved as if he was entitled to things.

"I'd never regret giving him something that makes him happy," Shane replied.

Shane won her heart with that. It was just that simple.

When the gifts were handed out, Shane was surprised there were several for him. That gave Shane additional courage to do what he felt he had to do.

He had yet to present Cris with his gift for her. Tucked away in his pocket, it seemed to grow heavier and heavier by the moment.

When the gathering began to break up, he stepped up to Cris. "Can I see you outside for a minute?"

She appeared a little torn as she looked down at her son. "Go," Richard urged. "I'll put Ricky to bed," he volunteered happily. "It's been a while since I read to him."

"Okay," Cris agreed. She paused to kiss her son on the head and said, "Listen to Grandpa." Then she turned toward Shane. "Lead the way."

He led her over to the side of the veranda. Once outside and alone, Cris asked, "Something wrong?"

"Nothing's wrong," he assured her. And then he took a breath, praying he wouldn't wind up tripping over his own tongue. He was more a man of action than words. The irony of the situation struck him just then. "You know, I told myself I wouldn't do this."

Cris still didn't understand what was going on or what he was getting at, although she knew in her heart what she *hoped* he was getting at.

"Do what?"

Here went nothing—or everything, he amended. "Wouldn't tell you how I felt about you. But a part of me is afraid that if I let this slip by, if I just remain silent and let things unfold along the path they're already on, I'll regret it not just for now or even later, but for the rest of my life."

Shane paused, almost afraid to continue. If he didn't say the words, didn't bare his soul to her, he couldn't hear her reject him if it came to that.

But he also wouldn't hear her say yes—if he got to be that lucky.

He dug into his pocket and pulled out the small silver-paper-wrapped box that had been burning a hole in his pocket and held out the box to her.

"Here."

She stared at the small gift, feeling numb with anticipation—yet afraid to find out what it was. Because what if it wasn't what she thought it was? Then she'd be devastated.

So instead of reaching for it, she asked softly, "What is it?"

"Open it," he urged.

Hands trembling, she took the little box from him and removed the wrapping paper. There was a velvet box inside it. Cris held her breath as she pushed back the lid.

"It's a ring," she whispered. A row of small diamonds winked at her, as if to share their secret with her. She looked up at Shane. Waiting.

"It was my mother's. Her wedding ring," he added needlessly. And then he plunged into the deep end of the pool by saying what was in his heart. "I want you to marry me. Or stay married to me, however you want to look at it." He was fumbling, he chided himself. Taking a breath, he tried again. "I've loved you since before you ever went out with Mike and I know I don't have the right to turn this charade to my advantage, but—"

He didn't get a chance to finish because Cris had thrown her arms around his neck and sealed her mouth to his even as tears began to stream down her face.

For a moment, Shane allowed the dizzying excitement to fill his being and take over. He kissed her back, losing himself in the blooming green fields of hope and the promise of a world of tomorrows.

When the kiss ended and she moved her head back, he was dazed enough to ask, "Is that a yes, or are you just trying not to hurt my feelings?"

She laughed then, laughed with happiness, laughed with relief and just plain joy. "Yes, that's a yes."

He still couldn't get himself to believe it. "A real yes, or a pity yes?"

"Will you just shut up and hold me?" she cried, laying her head against his chest.

"I can do that," he told her, closing his arms around her.

The sound of his heart beating against her cheek was the most reassuring sound she'd heard in a very long time. Cris was sorely tempted to remain like that indefinitely, until all the stars faded from the sky.

But ever the responsible one, she had a wedding to prepare for. Alex and Wyatt's wedding.

As she raised her head to look at Shane, something caught her attention. She'd barely glimpsed it out of the corner of her eye, but it was far too dramatic to dismiss.

It caused her to draw in her breath sharply in utter surprise.

Shane stiffened. "What is it?" he asked, looking around and not knowing just what to expect.

Cris pointed behind him. "Mama's azalea bush," she said in wonder. "It was in full bloom this morning. I thought it was Mama's way of saying she was happy about Alex finally marrying Wyatt. But look at it now!" she cried.

The azalea bush was the very last thing on his mind, but he knew how special that plant was to her. So he turned toward where the bush had been planted.

The bush was an explosion of blossoms and color. He'd never seen anything like it. "Is it supposed to do that?" he wanted to know.

"The blossoms have tripled in size." Smiling at him, she said, "You realize what that means?"

He took a guess grounded in fact. "Silvio overfertilized it?"

"No." She laughed. "It means that Mama's not just happy about Alex and Wyatt, but about us, too. I think she wants us to stay married."

He took Cris back into his arms. This was

going to work out, he told himself, finally beginning to relax. "Well, that makes two of us."

"Three," Cris corrected, her eyes dancing. "That makes three of us."

"Can't beat those odds," he agreed.

"Don't you even try," she told him just before he kissed her again.

EPILOGUE

"Well, we did it. We got them married," Richard announced happily.

He had come to the tiny private cemetery and he was standing between the headstones of his wife and his best friend.

Oh, their remains might be buried beneath his feet, but he knew Amy and Dan weren't really there. Their essence, the special thing that made them who they were, was all around him. Both were with him in spirit, and would be no matter where he might go.

"I wish you both could have been there—in fact as well as in spirit," he went on. "Alex made a beautiful bride, Amy. And Wyatt, Wyatt never looked handsomer, Dan. You would have been proud of them," he said. "They were a striking couple.

"But that we were all prepared for. The surprise," he continued with a smile, "was when Cris and Shane came down the aisle. Rather, when Cris came down the aisle after Alex to join Shane, who was standing beside Wyatt at the altar. I was as surprised as anyone when I saw them. Turns out it was all a last-minute thing—*really* last-minute," he emphasized.

Richard laughed, shaking his head. He was still a little stunned by it all.

"You know that marriage of convenience Cris and Shane had agreed to so she could to keep custody of Ricky? Seems those two really did have feelings for each other. Strong feelings that apparently blossomed into love when no one was watching.

"From what I gather," he continued, getting comfortable in his recitation, "Cris looked so wistful helping Alex into her dress that when she let slip she and Shane were staying married, Alex immediately suggested a double wedding. You know Cris— she doesn't like to fuss. But according to Stevi, the girls could all see how much she wanted to have a real wedding, with flowers and everything—you remember I told you she married her first husband in city hall, so the girl never had a proper wedding. Anyway, Alex, Stevi and Andy wouldn't take no for an answer. They got your wedding dress out of the attic and it fit Cris like a dream—"

Richard paused and sighed. "When the music played and I saw her walking down the aisle, it was almost like seeing you on our wedding day all over again—I can't begin to tell you how much I miss you, Amy."

His eyes were misting and he wiped his eyes with the tips of his fingers.

"I know, I know, I'm not supposed to get sentimental. But you two will have to cut me a little slack, here," he told them. "This has been a very emotional day.

"As for Shane—he's a fine man, Amy. You'd like him. Strong, handsome—reminds me a lot of myself when I was his age," Richard added with a chuckle. "Anyway, you'd think that he'd look out of place in the wedding party beside Wyatt, but that boy of yours, Dan, he's got a gift for making things happen. Managed to make a few phone calls, and before you know it, Shane is in a tux looking just as splendid as Wyatt. It was a sight that would have warmed any parent's heart. It certainly did mine." Richard beamed.

"So now it's done. Two down and two to go, Amy. Although between you and me, honey, whoever winds up with Stevi's going to have to have the patience of Job. She's a handful and she talks faster than anyone on my side of the family...." He trailed off and was silent for a moment. "I'm a lucky, lucky man, having those girls for daughters. The only thing that would have made me luckier is if you could have stayed just a little while longer, Amy. You, too, Dan." He looked at his best friend's headstone. "It gets lonely sometimes, not hearing your voices, being the only one doing all the talking. But I know what you'd both say."

He nodded.

"Yes, I'll carry on for the three of us until we can all be reunited again."

Richard looked toward the rear of the inn. He needed to be getting back before someone came looking for him.

"I'll keep you posted," he promised, and

turned, but glanced over his shoulder at the headstones one last time.

Then, with a smile, thinking of the family waiting for him at the reception, Richard began to walk slowly back along the winding path that led to the inn.

* * * * *

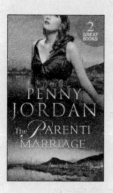

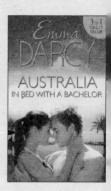

Discover more romance at

www.millsandboon.co.uk

- ❤ WIN great prizes in our exclusive competitions
- ❤ BUY new titles before they hit the shops
- ❤ BROWSE new books and REVIEW your favourites
- ❤ SAVE on new books with the Mills & Boon® Bookclub™
- ❤ DISCOVER new authors

PLUS, to chat about your favourite reads, get the latest news and find special offers:

- 📘 Find us on facebook.com/millsandboon
- 🐦 Follow us on twitter.com/millsandboonuk
- ❤ Sign up to our newsletter at millsandboon.co.uk